Rebellious

A Rebel Spinoff

By

Nona Day

Natavia Presents

Rebellious: A Rebel Spin-Off Nona Day

Introduction

Jiera

"**W**here is Lexi?" I asked panicking. Today was my wedding day and she wasn't here to do my makeup.

"Don't worry Jay. You know she's coming. Just relax," Tawny said stroking my back.

I was an emotional wreck. I was 7 months pregnant and getting married to the man of my dreams. I love King with every beat of my heart and from the depth of my soul. Even though, this was the best day of my life. I couldn't help but feel a sense of sadness. I didn't have anyone to walk me down the aisle. This was supposed to be Tone's job. I hated that he wasn't here to share this day with me. He's also missing the upcoming birth of his first child.

"I already look like a damn whale. I at least wanted to look cute," I said getting agitated.

Claudette laughed. "You are not even that big. Wait until next month. That's when you will blow up."

"Exactly, look at me," Toya said rubbing her belly. She was due any day now.

"That's comforting," I said rolling my eyes. They all laughed.

We were in the dressing room of the church. The church was decorated in tangerine, yellow and orange. Tulips of similar colors were placed throughout the church. Lexi was my maid of honor, while Claudette was my matron of honor. Tawny and Lexi were bridesmaid's. I hadn't seen King since last night. He celebrated his last night as a single man with his friends. I enjoyed a night on a party bus with my girls. We hit up bars, strip and night clubs, and casinos. We had a blast.

"Awww, look at you," Angela said walking into the room. She helped me choose my dress from her boutique. It was an ivory, A-line, V-neck, long chiffon gown. The top was beaded and laced while the bottom cascaded with ruffles.

I smiled at her. "Thank you." She hugged me tightly.

"You are so tense," she said.

"She's panicking because Lexi isn't here yet," Tawny said.

"Oh relax. She's coming. She's outside talking to Max," she told me stroking my arm.

"Ugh, I don't have time for their shenanigans," I said stomping toward the door to drag her in here. I know those two will end up arguing and destroying my day. There was a knock on the door. I breathed a sigh of relief knowing she was here.

"Come on in," Angela said.

I covered my mouth as it fell open and my eyes widened. I lost mobility in my legs. I don't know who caught me from falling to the ground. My eyes were fixated on the man standing in front of me. "Tone?" I heard Toya ask as she sobbed. She ran and wrapped her arms around him as she cried. I watched him hold her tightly with his face buried in her neck.

After a few minutes, she let him go. He pulled me into his arms. "What's up baby sis?" He said with a smile. He looked like my brother, the handsome one that I remembered before the drugs.

I cried. "I thought you were dead."

"Shit, I was. I was a walking damn zombie," he said.

"How are you here?" I asked.

He looked over his shoulder. I saw Max and Riley standing at the door. "They spared my life. I couldn't return until I got my shit together. I've been clean since that day. I'm going to stay that way. I promise." I wrapped my arms around his neck and cried.

"I just found out a couple of hours ago. So, get all the crying out the way so I can get to work," she said sitting her bag on the table.

"Where's King? Does he know about this?" I asked with concern. If he didn't, he would for sure kill Tone on our wedding day.

"It was his decision. He's waiting to see you come down the aisle," Tone said. More tears poured down my face.

After calming my emotions, Lexi finally did my makeup. I didn't think this day could get any better, but King made it possible. I don't know what made him spare Tone's life, but I'm so grateful he did. The church doors opened for me to walk in. King stood at the front of the church with Max, Riley, and Daryll. He looked so handsome standing in his ivory tuxedo. Tone walked me down the aisle to marry the man that would hold my heart forever.

Lexi

Over a year later

"**G**et the hell out Maxwell! You don't get to fuck everything with a vagina and control who comes and goes in my house," I told Max as we stood in the middle of my condo. One of his birds had sent me a picture of him asleep in her bed through my Facebook messenger. I knew the picture was recent because of the new tattoo on his upper shoulder. He had just gotten it a few days ago.

"This isn't a house," he said with a smirk. He purchased this condo for me a few months ago. He never reminded me that he brought this place for me when I throw him out.

"Ugh! Just leave! I have to get ready for work," I said walking into my bedroom.

"Why you always letting that bullshit get to you? "They just doing that shit to break us up."

"You just don't get it! Well, it fucking worked," I screamed at him.

"Who that nigga was leaving here?" He asked leaning against the bedroom door frame.

"None of your business," I said taking off my clothes to get in the shower. The guy was at the wrong apartment door, but I wasn't going to tell him that. I wanted him to think there was someone else.

He chuckled. "I see him here again, he's dead."

"Stay away from him. I don't run up on the thots and birds you fucking," I demanded.

"Man, them bitches don't mean shit to me. You know you the only one I got love for," he said staring at me.

I simply shook my head and walked into bathroom. I'm so over dealing with him and his hoeish ways. It's been a year since we decided to end our relationship. The only problem is Max still thinks he can control what goes on in my life. Every guy he sees me with he makes it his personal mission to run them in the opposite direction. I know it's my fault for allowing him to come and go whenever he pleases. I try to stay strong whenever he comes around, but it's just so hard. He's just so damn irresistible, sexy and crazy. That's a perfect combination to me. The closer I tried getting to Max he would push me away. After a while, I became tired of trying to get him to love me like I love him. I made the decision to let him go and try to be his friend. Just the sight of him causes my panties to become soaked.

"Yo Lexi," he said as I turn to face him.

"What?" I asked with an attitude.

"You still love me?" He asked with a smirk.

"Fuck you and good bye," I said before closing the bathroom door. I could hear him laughing which only irritated me more.

After showering, I dressed and headed to work. I had a great job as a RN at an assisted living facility. The best thing I loved about my job were the elderly residents. They gave me so much wisdom about life and lessons. I walked into the breakroom to find everyone laughing until they were in tears.

"Drea, what's going on?" I asked my coworker.

"Girl, that freaky ass Ms. V," she said wiping the tears from her cheeks.

"What has she done?" I asked with a smile.

"She got caught giving Mr. Harold head in the room last night," she said laughing.

I burst out laughing. Ms. V was my favorite resident. She is a wealthy, overweight, elderly, Caucasian lady that loves sex. This isn't the first time she was caught having sex with another resident. Residents had their own private room, so I had no idea why they were in the laundry room.

"Mr. Harold is married," I said more to myself.

"Yes, her and Mrs. Sandy were fighting in the game room an hour ago," Angie said still laughing. "Ms. V pulled Mrs. Sandy wig off and slung it across the room. Mrs. Sandy pulled a Van Dame move on her with a karate kick knocking her big ass on the floor. Girl, I swear the floor shook."

"Oh my God! They are too old for that," I said laughing.

"Yes, but you couldn't tell they are damn near in their 80's this morning," she said.

"Is Ms. V okay?" I asked with concern.

"Chile yea, talking about she going to sue Mrs. Sandy," Angie said shaking her head.

"Let me go make my rounds and check on my girl," I said.

"With her hoe ass," Angie said. "This has been an entertaining day. I picked up a shift last night since I was off today."

I laughed. "Ok, have a good day."

After making my daily rounds, I went to Ms. V's room. She was sitting in her recliner watching television. "I hear you've been misbehaving young lady."

She smiled. "That old bitch tried me. She can't get mad because her husband wants this wet."

I burst into laughter. "Ms. V you are a mess."

"What are you looking stressed about? You still letting that boy run you crazy?" She asked staring at me. I just shook my head. "You better get you some young, good dick on the side. Don't wait around on that fool to treat you right." I knew everything she was saying was the truth. It's just so much easier to say than do.

"I hear everything you're saying Ms. V, but it's not that easy. How do you let go of someone you love?" I asked with sadness.

"Realize that loving them isn't worth sacrificing your own happiness and peace," she said with soft eyes. I nodded my head in agreement.

Max

"Where the fuck Maxi, Cherry?" I asked with anger.

Cherry was always on some bullshit. Cherry was pregnant with Maxi when I went down. Riley and King made sure she was taken care of until I was released. It was the greatest moment of my life when I laid eyes on my little girl. I would never let Cherry bring her to visit me. I didn't want my baby girl visiting a prison. Cherry and I were never a couple. We just fucked around from time to time. She didn't know I knew she was fucking some little, young corner hustler while I was locked up. He was going around bragging about how she was giving him money and shit. I didn't even let her know when I was being released. I surprised her the evening of my release date. Riley gave me a key since he was paying her rent. I walked in the house to find her sucking the nigga dick in the shower. I ran both their asses out the house butt ass naked covered with soap suds. Just for the fun of it, I ran his naked ass around the block with my new truck Riley had copped for me. From that moment on, Cherry was only good for fucking and sucking. I always made sure my baby was well provided for, but Cherry couldn't get shit from me.

"She with Sherry," she said. I hated that broad shouldered hoe too. She was one of Riley's ex birds that's always causing drama. Lately her and Cherry been joined at the hip.

Natavia Presents

"Why the fuck you call me over here if Maxi isn't here?" I asked looking at her as she lay across her bed. It was obvious what she wanted since she only had on a thong and tank top.

"I thought maybe we could spend some time together. You haven't blessed me with some of that good dick in a while," she said giving a seductive stare.

I couldn't deny how sexy she was. Cherry was a brown skinned beauty. She was short, slender with perfect curves. She wore her hair with different weaves. Today she was rocking some long weave. I could feel my dick getting hard as I stared down at her. She sat up and scooted to the edge of the sofa. She unfastened my jeans and pulled my hard dick out. My shit started throbbing as she massaged it with her hand. I closed my eyes and Lexi's pretty ass face was looking at me.

"Come on Daddy. Bless me with some of that good ass dick," she said looking up at me.

"Nah, suck that shit," I said staring down at her. She smiled and went to work. I kept my eyes open not wanting to see the face of the woman whose heart I keep breaking. I gripped a handful of her hair and fucked her mouth until I unloaded. I once cared about Cherry. King had informed me that she tried to fuck him when I was locked up. If she wanted to pass it to the homie it was cool with me. She just shouldn't expect me to love her. I went to the bathroom and washed my dick off. She was laying across the bed with a frown on her face.

"Call me when my daughter comes home," I said looking down at her.

"Are you ever going to forgive me?" She asked looking up at me.

I laughed. "Nah Ma, we are co-parents. That's all the forgiveness I can give you."

"Nigga, you were cheating on me before you got sent up. Don't act like you were the faithful boyfriend," she said with an attitude.

"First of all, we were never a couple. I was always straight up with you. Secondly, you are right. You are free to fuck and suck whoever you choose. Just don't expect any type of love from me. To be honest with you Cherry, this shit between us been over. I don't know why we still fucking around," I told her.

"Because you love this good pussy," she said with a smile.

I shook my head and chuckled. "Nah, trust me that's not it."

"Oh, you saying my pussy ain't good?" she said sitting up in the bed.

"Shit, it ain't the best I done had," I said with a smile.

"I guess that yellow bitch still got you in your feelings," she said with a smirk.

I smiled at her. She couldn't stand Lexi, because she knew how I felt about her. "Yea, she does." I winked at her and walked out the bedroom.

The connection to Cherry was history. We were both doing our own thang, but held a level of respect for each other. Cherry was still out there fucking every nigga she can to keep money in her pockets. I wasn't one to stop her hustle and I damn sure wasn't one to put my heart into her hoe ass. After leaving Cherry's house, I went to check on my grandmother. She shared my heart with Maxi and Lexi. She raised me from the age of thirteen years old. I was eleven years old when my mother left me with my father. The thought of that nigga brought nothing but hate into my heart. He had a heart attack in prison. I only regretted I couldn't spit in his face before he died.

"Hi baby," Granny said giving me a hug when I walked in the kitchen. I gave her a hug and kiss on the cheek.

"What are you cooking?" I asked.

"Some chicken and rice," she said.

"Hell yea, a nigga hungry too," I said rubbing my stomach.

"Boy, watch your mouth," she said hitting me upside the head. "Sit down, I'll fix your plate. I just finished."

I sat at the kitchen table and start eating the moment she sat the plate in front of me. She hit me across the head again, but harder this time.

"What you do that for Granny?" I asked massaging the back of my head.

"Say your blessings before you eat a meal the good Lord has blessed you with," she said.

I smiled at her. "My bad." Granny was very religious. She didn't play about disrespecting our God. I said my prayers and started eating again.

"Your mother called the other day," she said sitting at the table.

I felt a sickness in my stomach. "Granny not while I'm eating."

"She wants to see you," she said touching my hand.

"Nah, I'm good," I said.

"I'm not going to force you to see her, but you need to Max. You have so much anger inside you. Say your peace to her," she advised me.

"I'll think about it," I lied just to get off the subject.

"Good, now where my other two babies?" She asked smiling at me.

"Two?" I asked confused. Granny was getting up in age, so I know her mind might be getting forgetful.

"Yes, Maxi and Lexi," she said with a grin.

I chuckled. She was crazy about Lexi. Lexi would sit and talk to her for hours. She takes Granny shopping and even goes to church with her since I don't anymore. "Maxi hanging with one of Cherry's friends. Lexi ain't feeling me right now."

She shook her head. "You gone mess around and lose that girl. You keep on holding everything inside. Let her in Maxwell. Allow yourself to love her the way she loves you."

"I hear you Granny," I said. If only it was as easy to do as it is to say.

And stop fooling with that jezebel, Cherry. I never liked that lil pigeon toed heifer." I burst into laughter. She wasn't lying. She never liked Cherry.

"I hear you Granny," I said as I continued to eat.

I understood everything she was saying to me was the truth. I just wasn't ready to pour my heart and inner demons out to Lexi or anyone else. My heart and mind were dedicated to the streets. My only concern was making money and gaining power. I knew I was taking a risk at losing Lexi. I could see it in her eyes and feel it in her touches that she was tired of my selfishness. I couldn't open myself up to talk about all that shit I went through. I also couldn't bear the thought of another man loving her. I just didn't know how to let her go.

<u>Riley</u>

Since King stepped down and we took over his father's empire, business in the streets is bringing in more money than we can count. Life seems to be moving fast now. I'm thinking about following in King's footsteps and settling down with Tawny. I love her chocolate sexy ass more than she knows. It just seems we never have time for each other. I'm running the streets and my legit business and she's building her successful dance studio. Her birthday is next weekend, so I've decided to take her on a much-needed vacation as a surprise. It was time we spent some time only focusing on us. I knew I could leave Max to handle business. His head was so damn deep in the game he couldn't see what he was losing in the process.

"What up," King said opening his front door. We were all having dinner at their house. Jiera was working her ass off at the boutique, taking care of their little boy, Mufasa. King was adamant about stopping his father's name with him, so he didn't give him his name. Jiera refused to hire anyone to cook and clean the house. The only help she would allow was Angela, King's mother.

"Shit, ready for a good home cooked meal," I said walking in rubbing my stomach.

He chuckled. "Tawny ain't cooking for your ass?"

"Man, we hardly see each other lately," I said shaking my head.

He looked at me with his head tilted and raised brow. "What's up with that?"

"Nah, nothing like that. We both just consumed with work," I said.

"Oh ok," he said with a smile.

"I'm taking her to Jamaica next weekend for her birthday," I told him.

"Good, don't be out there fucking up like Max," he said with a laugh.

"Yea, that fool ain't thinking about slowing down," I said shaking my head.

"That's because he doesn't think he has anything to lose. When reality slaps his ass in the face he's going to be a sick lonely dog," King said as we walked into the den.

"He's coming over," I informed him.

"Oh shit, I hope him, and Lexi don't start all that arguing," he said with a laugh.

"Get your son King, he needs changing," Jiera said walking into the den holding Mufasa. He was the chubbiest, cutest little boy with features of both King and Jiera.

"Oh, he my son with he's shitty?" King said taking the baby in his arms.

"You got that right," Jiera said tiptoeing and kissing King on the cheek. They were still like damn horny teenagers around each other.

"Oh, yea Riley where's Tawny?" She asked walking over to me.

"She's on her way," I said giving her a hug.

"Damn, are you going to let her go?" King asked staring at me. Jiera and I burst into laughter. He was still possessive and crazy as hell about her.

King tapped her on the ass as she walked out the den. She giggled and kept walking. King changed Mufasa's diaper and fussed the entire time about the smell. The baby just giggled and swayed his short, chubby legs in the air. Looking at King and his son was making me want to start my own family with Tawny.

I was raised in a big family. I have three sisters and two brothers. My twin sisters are still at home with my parents. They'll be graduating from high school this year. I was raised in a stable home with loving parents. I just loved the street life. My dad ran his own landscaping company. My mom has always worked at home. She took care of home, while my father took care of the bills. They were still very happy with their lives. I hope to one day build what they have. I bump heads with my parents all the time about my dealings in the streets. They'll never understand how addictive this fast money is to me. I never argue with them when they voice their opinions, because at the end of the day I'm still going to be chasing the paper. Tawny and I have never discussed kids. I know I want some, I'm not sure if she does. I know she loves spending time with Mufasa, but I don't know if she was ready for her own child. I guess that will be a conversation we will have on our vacation.

"How is the business going?" King asked sitting Mufasa down on the floor. He came crawling toward me. I lifted him up and started playing with him. He laughed and cooed as I made silly faces at him. "You are real comfortable over there."

I looked at King and shrugged my shoulders. "It's about that time. Shit, I don't want to be an old man trying to enjoy my kids."

"I feel ya. That's why I'm trying to pump another one in Jiera now," he said with a smile.

I laughed. "Jay ain't hearing that shit."

He smiled. "Before this year is over, I bet she'll be pregnant again."

I only laughed. I wasn't stupid enough to bet him. I'm sure he'll have Jay pregnant just like he said. Those two were just like horny ass rabbits. We started discussing business projects we wanted to do together. King didn't want to know anything going on the streets. He only wanted to be informed if his help was needed. I knew I would never come to him even if we did need help unless I had to. My brother was living the life he wanted. I had no plans of disrupting that. Besides everything in the streets was running well. The only problem we were having right now was finding places to hide all the money coming in. Daryll was coming over for dinner to give us some ideas on washing our dirty money.

<u>Tawny</u>

I'm so ready for this vacation next weekend with Riley. We haven't been able to spend much time together the last few months. My dance studio has exploded with business lately. It didn't help that I decided to take on more classes. Riley was not happy about that at all. I had no choice because the few classes I was giving wasn't enough. I loved what I was doing and had no plans of slowing down. I knew what my goal was the first day I graduated high school. Stripping was only a stepping stone to what I wanted to accomplish. I worked too hard to slow down when everything is falling into place for me. After I decided to hire a couple of instructors, Riley calmed down about the additional classes. Now, I had to muster up the courage to tell him I was considering opening another studio. I decided I will discuss it with him while he's relaxed on our vacation. I had just arrived at King and Jiera's house for dinner. King opened the door to let me in.

"Damn, I thought my boy was going to have to go find yo ass," he said opening the door.

"Hush King, I'm not that late," I said gently pushing him out the way. "Where's everyone?"

"Yo man and Max in the den. Jiera in the kitchen still cooking," he said leading me to the den.

I walked into the den to see Riley sitting on the sofa looking so damn handsome and sexy. His light tan skin was covered with beautiful tattoos. He wore his beard and mustache trimmed very low. It didn't take a genius to tell he was biracial. His Latino, Caucasian, Irish and African American genes meshed perfectly together. He smiled at me showing his perfect white teeth as I walked toward him. I always loved the way his eyes roamed all over my body. "Hey baby, sorry I'm a little late."

I leaned down and kissed his soft lips. He pulled me down on his lap sliding his tongue into my mouth. I could only moan softly and enjoy the taste of his minty breath with a twist of Hennessey. "You good sexy," he said after breaking our kiss.

"Y'all can stop all that shit. Show some restraint in other people's home," Max said looking at us both.

"Man, you shut the hell up. You and Lexi ass slipped into our damn private room and fucked," King said mean mugging Max.

Max smiled. "I've apologized repeatedly about that. She needed some "act right.""

"Where is she anyway?" I asked looking around. Max shrugged his shoulders. I knew he had done something to piss her off again. "Where's my precious little Godson?"

"You just missed him. Ma wanted to keep him tonight," King said with a devilish smile on his face.

"What are you smiling like that for?" I asked staring at him.

"Ma just plowed the field, so I can plant my seeds again," he said with a big smile. Riley and Max burst into laughter. Their baby wasn't a year old and he was trying to get Jiera pregnant again.

I giggled and shook my head. "I'm going in the kitchen to see if she needs help. I know she has some wine for me."

"Yea, I'm tired of y'all stealing my shit," King said as I walked out the den. We stayed stealing his expensive liquor and wine.

"Lil Mama got it smelling good in here," I said walking in the kitchen.

"Hey girl, I was wondering was I going to have to deal with those fools by myself," she said looking over her shoulder.

"I had to go home and change first. I was too sweaty. You need some help?" I asked.

"Yes, I do. You can cut up those vegetables for me," she said pointing at the kitchen isle.

"I need a glass of wine first," I said pouring myself a glass. "Girl, how do you have time to cook and run the store?"

"It was hard at first. I didn't know if I would be able to do it all when I went back to work after having Mufasa. King kept trying to get me to hire someone to help around the house. You know I wasn't hearing that shit. Hire some lil old lady, then her pretty ass granddaughter happens to stop by one day...nah, I'll pass," Jiera said before taking a sip from her glass. "So, I hired a manager at the store."

I laughed. "Smart move." We toasted and chugged the glasses down only to refill them. "Where the hell is Lexi?"

"Her and Max at each other throats again," she said shaking her head.

I shook mine along with her. "Those two can't work it out, but can't stand to be apart." We chatted while we finished cooking. We didn't get to see much of each other like we use to, so when we did get together we talked nonstop. We all understand we had busy lives and we couldn't spend as much time together, but we were all there for each other if anyone of use just needed to vent. Right now, it seems we need to find Lexi and let her relieve her frustrations.

Lexi

"Hi sis, I didn't know you were going to be here," I said walking in my parent's house. I had an exhausting day at work. All I wanted to do was go home and climb in my bed. I was supposed to be going over to King and Jiera's house for dinner, but I was in no mood to deal with Max tonight. As I was getting off from work Drea, my co-worker text me that she saw Max leaving Cherry's apartment. I knew he wasn't there seeing Maxi, because Sherry had posted pictures of her and Maxi at Chucky Cheese. I knew Sherry was only trying to impress Riley by spending time with Maxi. She still thinks she stands a chance with him. *Delusional ass.*

"I just stopped by before heading home. I got a couple of heads to braid," she said.

"I don't know why you don't get your own shop. You make more money doing hair than being a nurse," I told her.

"Ssshhh, you know we can't discuss our dreams and aspirations in this house," she said jokingly with a whisper. Even though she was joking, she was telling the truth. Our parents mapped our lives out for us. We were to be nurses or doctors. Our two older sisters were happy with their careers as nurses. One is continuing her education to become a plastic surgeon. Aisha and I wanted different things in life. I wanted to do makeup. We would discuss opening our own business together in private. When we discussed the idea with our parents, they acted as if we told them we wanted to be prostitutes. They had no idea I stripped before getting my RN license. We wanted our father's approval so much we agreed to their plans with our lives. Now that we are older, we wanted to make our own decisions. The problem was we were too afraid to tell them.

"I'm not staying. I just come to see what Ma cooked," I told her.

"Nothing, that's why I stopped by. They have a dinner party to attend," she informed me.

"Well damn, I guess I'm going home to get dressed and go over to King and Jiera's house for dinner," I said. I was in no mood to cook.

"You aren't going to say hi before you go?" she asked looking up at me.

"I'll come by tomorrow. I'm not in the mood for one of those speeches about following in our older sisters' footsteps," I said. The only time my father gave me attention was when he was giving me a speech about my future. I was in no mood to deal with it today either.

"Yea, because they have careers, husbands and children," Aisha said mocking my dad. Aisha and I never got much attention from our father. It seemed we were always doing extra things to impress him, but nothing measured up to what our older sisters did.

After slipping out the house, I hurried home to get dressed. I decided to invite a friend to come with me. If Max thought I was going to sit around and wait for him to love me, he was highly mistaken. Randall was a physician assistant at the living facility where I work. He had been trying to get me to go out on a date with him for the longest. I figured this would be a nice way to get to know him without the measure of being alone with him. Randall was not my type. I decided it was time for me to try a different type. The type of men I was attracted to just didn't seem to be working out for me. He was tall, dark and handsome and carried himself with class. He was what you would call "a distinguished gentleman." He was a confident and charismatic. He dressed well and had perfect manners.

Once we arrived at the house, I rang the doorbell. A couple of minutes later Jiera opened the door and her eyes nearly popped out her head. She stood there staring at me in disbelief. "JR, are you going to invite us in?"

"Oh, I'm sorry. Come in. I didn't think you were going to make it. I'm just surprised to see you," she said stepping out the way to let us in. We gave each other a hug.

"Well, I changed my mind. I decided I'd bring Randall with me to taste your delicious cooking. You remember meeting him," I said with a smile.

"Yes, he works with you right?"

"Yes, I finally convinced her to spend some time with me outside of work," Randall said putting his hand around my waist. I hated that I didn't get that tingling feeling that Max gives me whenever he touches me. I forced a smile as I looked up at him.

"We were just getting ready to sit down and eat," Jiera said with a concerned look on her face. I knew she was worried about Max seeing me with Randall. I didn't give a damn knowing he was fucking Cherry earlier today.

"I brought this bottle of wine for you ladies to enjoy," Randall said giving her the wine.

"Oh wow, thank you," Jiera said taking the bottle from him.

We followed Jiera into the dining room where everyone was seated. They all looked up at us and it was as if you could hear a pin drop. My eyes immediately connected with Max and I knew I had made a mistake by inviting Randall with me. His eyes showed no emotion as he stared at me. "No fucking up shit in my house tonight. Let's all act got damn civilized," King said standing up.

<u>Max</u>

I can't lie she hit a soft spot showing up with another nigga in my presence, but I'm not going to give her what she wants. She wants a reaction out of me. I was tempted to give her one by choking the hell out of her pretty ass, but I remained seated. Lexi and her date sat across the table from me. I kept my eyes focused on her. I wanted her to look me in the eyes, but she never did. She spoke to everyone and introduced her date to us all. I knew everyone was waiting on me to react. I did the opposite of what they all expected. I shook Randall's hand with a smile. Lexi was an attention seeker. This was her way of trying to get under my skin. We all sat, ate and made small talk. The nigga kept leaning over whispering in Lexi's ear. It was time to put an end to the shit.

"Yo Randall, you like fruit?" I asked. Everyone looked at me with a puzzled look.

"I think everyone enjoys some type of fruit," Randall answered before taking a sip of his wine.

"Do you like watermelon? You don't look like a man that likes to eat watermelon," I said with a smile. I could see Lexi starting to fidget in her seat. I always told her she tastes like watermelon, my favorite fruit.

"You are right. I don't eat any melons."

"Damn, that's too bad. I love watermelon," I said staring at Lexi and licking my lips. I could hear King and Riley chuckle. Lexi gulped down her glass of wine and refilled her glass. Randall had a confused look on his face.

"Lexi, are you taking the trip with us tomorrow?" Tawny asked trying to change the subject.

"What trip?" King asked looking at Jiera.

She became nervous. "She wants us to go with her for a bachelorette party. They want strip dancing lessons. I was going to discuss it with you tonight King."

"Nah, I had plans for us tomorrow," King said shaking his head.

Jiera shrugged her shoulders. "I guess I won't have to use you tonight to practice some of the moves I wanted to show the girls tomorrow."

King cleared his throat. "We'll discuss it later." Jiera smiled, because she knew she had hoodwinked his ass. We all laughed.

"Pussy whipped ass," I said under my breath. I knew he heard me.

"At least I'm going to be the one in that pussy tonight unlike you," he said in a low voice. I chuckled.

"Yes, I'm going," Lexi answered.

"What do you do Tawny?" Randall asked looking at Tawny.

"I own a strip and pole dancing studio. I've recently added a dance section for young girls," Tawny answered.

"You are a stripper?" Randall asked turning his eyes to Lexi.

"I was," Lexi answered with no shame. I always told her never be ashamed of her past or current life.

"Wow, I had no idea," the cornball replied. He had better not look at her any differently than he was looking when he walked in here with her or he'll be limping out.

"Well, I'm glad you decided you wanted more for yourself. You are so much more than a stripper," he said.

"Nigga, didn't you just hear my girl say she owns a strip dancing school. Don't disrespect her occupation," Max said staring him down.

"I'm sorry. I didn't mean to degrade her in any way."

"So, you work together?" King asked Lexi and the cornball she had with her.

"Yes, I'm a PA. I've pursued this little feisty beauty from the first day I saw her. She finally decided to give me a chance," he said smiling at Lexi. She blushed nervously as she glanced at me.

"Have you fucked her yet?" I asked as I kept my eyes on Lexi. Her eyes nearly popped out her head. I didn't give a damn. I was done playing this childish ass game with her.

"Excuse me?" Randall asked looking at me.

I turned my eyes to him. "I asked have you fucked her yet. Before you answer you should know your life depends on the way you answer the question." Lexi jumped up from her seat and stormed out of the dining room. Without saying a word, I followed behind Lexi. I found her in the guest bathroom crying. She was wiping her tears looking in the mirror. I locked the bathroom door and sat on the toilet.

"You are a narcissistic asshole," she said with anger turning to face me.

"And that nigga is a cornball," I said with a smile.

"He's a damn gentleman that treats me with respect. That's more than you've ever offered," she said with an attitude.

She always looks sexy as hell when she is angry. Her skirt was hugging her petite frame perfectly. Lately she's been developing curves she never had. All I wanted to do was bury my dick deep inside her wet pussy. "Come here."

"No Maxwell, it's over. I'm not doing this with you anymore," she stated.

I couldn't stand the thought of not having her. Her not being mine was not an option for her or me. I stood up and pinned her against the bathroom counter. "You done with me Lexi?" I whispered in her ear as my hands roamed over her thighs and plump ass.

"Maxwell stop," she demanded with her soft face. I could tell she was trying to control herself, but I wasn't going to allow it. She belonged to me now and forever. That's some shit she might as well deal with.

The more I nibbled on her ear and caressed her body with my hands her breathing became shallow. I slowly started pushing her skirt up her thighs as I kissed all over her neck. I reached under her skirt tearing her lace panties off. She started wrestling with my jeans to get them unfastened. We were both breathing heavy as we tore each other clothes off. "Aaaahh yes Max," she whimpered as I licked and sucked her ample breast. She had just the right amount that satisfied me. I cupped both in my hands to give them an equal amount of attention. She moaned out loud when I softly bit her hard nipple. I lapped my tongue around the perfect tan circles on her breast. She pressed the back of my head to bury my face against her succulent breast.

I sat her on the counter and pulled her forward. For a moment, neither one of us moved. We just stared into each other's eyes. I loved Lexi in ways that I didn't know how to express to her other than sexually. The look in her eyes was pleading with me to reciprocate her love for me. "You'll always belong to me Lexi. I can't let you go," I said as I slid inside her soaked tight pussy. I couldn't hold the grunt from escaping my throat as her wet walls gripped my dick. She wrapped her toned legs around my waist while wrapping her arms around my neck. I started sliding in and out of her wetness and she whimpered and moaned.

"Oooh yes baby, don't stop," she moaned in my ear causing my dick to spread even more inside her. Her melon flavored juices were spilling unto the bathroom counter.

"Who pussy this is Lexi?" I said as I started thrusting deeper inside her.

"Fuucck! It's your baby! Shit, go deeper! This dick so damn good!" She moaned as she started gyrated her hips causing my dick to go deeper inside her.

I gripped her ass cheeks and started plummeting inside my pussy. She felt so damn good that my mouth started to water. I wanted to taste all the wetness she was spilling on my dick. Just when I was about to pull out and feast on her sweet pussy we were interrupted. "I swear to God I'm banning y'all from our damn house. Get the fuck outta there!" King demanded while banging on the door.

"Man hold the fuck up!" I roared back at him. "Damn!" I said trying to pull out of Lexi.

"Hell, fuck no! Finish what you damn started Maxwell!" she demanded gripping my dick and twirling her hips. She started kissing and licking on my neck. I don't know what it was about that shit, but it was my damn weakness. I started thrusting faster and deeper inside her. Her juices were sliding down my thighs as I slammed in and out of her. Sweat poured over our bodies as we held on to each other.

"Shit, this pussy feels good!" I barked feeling my nut trying to spill inside her.

"Oh God yes! I'm cooommming!" She screamed as her cream splattered all over the both of us.

"Shiiiiiitttt!" I groaned as I followed behind her spilling all my love inside her.

I held on to her as she rested her head on my shoulder. We both were silent trying to catch our breath. "I love you Maxwell."

"Shit Lexi, you know how a nigga feel about you. That shit ain't never changing." I meant every word I said to her. I knew Lexi was the one for me, I just didn't know how to be what she wanted me to be.

"You think he's still out there?" She asked about the cornball.

"Nah, but if he is I hope he heard you screaming," I said holding her tighter.

She giggled. "Let's get cleaned up and get out of here."

<u>Tone</u>

"I'll be here for a while Toya, but I'm not moving back. I have something good going on where I'm at," I explained to Toya as we sat in the restaurant eating lunch.

"What about your child and me?"

"The offer still stands for you to move to Minnesota. I would love to have my daughter with me," I told her.

"What about me, Tone? Do you want me there?"

"I offered for you to come stay, didn't I?" I asked. I do love Toya. I just wasn't sure I was ready to settle down with her. She was there for me during the roughest time of my life. I couldn't never turn my back on her. I'll do whatever I can to give her and my daughter the best that I can in life.

"Why can't you find a job here?" She asked. She didn't want to move to Minnesota. She said she loved Las Vegas and didn't want to move away. There were things I loved and missed about my hometown, but I loved my new life. "Maybe King can help you find something."

I chuckled. "The only reason I'm alive is because of his love for my sister. I'm not going to ask that man for a damn thing after what I did to them. I don't want to move back here Toya. Besides I don't have just a job, my Unc left me his company."

My uncle owned an electrical business. He passed away unexpectedly four months ago. He had already told me he was leaving me the business. I started working with him the moment I arrived there. We became close over the time he was alive. He had obtained a big contract for a hotel that was being built here before he passed. He had taught me a lot about the business since I moved with them. Getting over my addiction was a battle that I will never forget. I knew if I didn't stay off the drugs that King would kill me. I wasn't ready to leave this world. I needed to correct the wrongs I made with Jiera, Toya and Tawny. Tawny was the first and only girl I truly loved. She was there with me when I didn't have shit to offer her. I watched her grow as I dwindled to nothing and I could never stand it. I knew she would eventually realize she deserved more than I could give her. I tried to tear her down, so she wouldn't leave me instead I pushed her into the arms of another man. Over the past year, I've only visited home twice. I would come and spend time with my daughter, Jiera and my little chubby nephew. Seeing how happy she was with her life was a healing to my heart. I knew I had hurt her in a way that only true love can forgive. As far as Tawny, that's a wound that will never heal for me.

"Have you seen Jay yet?" She asked.

"Nah, she went out of town. She's going to stop by later this evening when she gets back," I informed her.

"She's so happy being married. Are we going to get married Tone?"

I took a deep breath. "I'm just getting my life back together. Right now, my focus is on building a better life for myself, so I can provide for my daughter the way she deserves."

"I'm not going to wait forever Tone," she said staring at me. Toya was a pretty girl. She resembled Keisha Knight-Pulliam. I just didn't love her enough to consider marrying her. At this point in my life I wasn't focused on anyone but myself. If she couldn't understand that, I wish her all the best in finding someone that could offer her what I couldn't now.

"Don't hold your life up for me Toya. I just want you to know I'll always be here for you whether we are together or not. You know my lil princess will always be well taken care of. I'll make sure of that," I told her.

"Stop talking like we are breaking up or something," she said smiling.

"Let's get out of here. A nigga ready to break your back," I said with a smile. She blushed and giggled.

Since her sister agreed to keep Lucindy for us, I had the entire night to release a lot of built up tension. She agreed to let me name our little girl after my mother. Regardless of the mistakes my mother made, she was a good mother to me and Jiera. I'm sure my biological father got in her head the same way he did mine. I regret the day I laid eyes on him.

"Yo get up. We need you to take a ride with us," the tall, muscular man said to me as I sat in the strip club high as hell.

"Man, I don't fucking know you. You interrupted my damn high," I said staring up at him.

"You either get your coked-up ass up or I'll drag your bitch ass out of here," he warned me.

"Nigga fuck you! Ain't no bitch in my blood," I stated. *This nigga had muscles like hulk, but I didn't give a fuck. High as I was I thought I could beat the nigga. He yanked me up by my arm and I swung on him with the other one. The nigga was so big he probably didn't feel it. He felt it when I bust the beer pitcher across his head though. After that I started kicking and stomping him until security pulled me off him. The next thing I know I was being thrown in the back of a limousine.*

I don't know how long we were riding before we pulled up to a huge ass mansion. I had no clue what business I could possibly have here. I didn't know anyone on this level. I only knew nickel and dime niggas. The big bear looking fool and another husky guy pulled me out the back seat. They lead me up the stairs and inside the double doors. After walking down, a long hall we entered an enormous study that could fit my small ass apartment inside it. I stared into the face of King Owens wondering what the hell did he want with me.

"Damn, what happened to you?" He asked looking at the oversized bear looking fool.

The other husky guy laughed. "He let this lil bitch ass nigga whoop his ass."

"I'll do the same for your ugly ass, call me a bitch again," I said staring at him.

"Y'all get the fuck out of here and let me talk to my guest," he ordered the two men.

After the men left, he went on to introduce himself. He started telling me how he gained his empire and how his son wanted to take it all from him. I knew he supplied just about every drug dealer in Vegas and surrounding cities. I knew of his reputation. I just wondered what he wanted with me. I sat and listened as he told the story of him and my mom. I wanted to kill the nigga for spitting lies out his mouth about my mother, but I knew I wouldn't make it out the house alive. After I argued with him about his lies, he wanted to prove me wrong. He asked me to go take a blood test with him the next day. I didn't see what he could benefit from me being his son, so I agreed to go. A couple of weeks later, I found out I was indeed his son. It took me a while to come to grips with that shit. My whole life was a lie. I already wasn't shit, now I wasn't shit without an identity. It didn't take much for him to convince me to help him bring down King. At the time King was the nigga I hated most. I spent a couple of weeks getting to know my biological father, the man that I thought wanted to have me as his son. It didn't take long for me to figure out, I was only a pawn in his game.

Natavia Presents

<u>Tawny</u>

"**O**oooh yes! Damn Ry please don't stop! I'm about to come," I screamed as I held on to the back of Riley's head as he sucked and slurped on my swollen clit. Slurping and smacking sounds bounced off the walls of my bedroom as he grunted and growled while devouring my essence. He slid two fingers inside me, causing me to almost pass out. My eyes rolled to the back of my head as my body quaked. I exploded like a torrential rain. He pulled his fingers out and continued licking and sucking as my body felt like it was elevated in the air. Tears started to fall down my face from the unimaginable pleasure that he always gives me.

Once he was done feasting on my juices, he flipped me over on all four. I spread my legs and gave him the perfect arch for him to enter me. "Damn, you always know how to sit that sweet pussy up right for me," he said sliding his ten-inch, thick dick inside me.

"Aaaaahhhh," we both moaned loudly together as he entered me. "Damn, I miss this pussy girl."

"We miss you too baby," I whimpered as he long stroked me from the back hitting every spot inside me. Sweat poured over my body as goosebumps popped up all over my flesh. Tingling sensations ran down my spine as he drilled inside me while massaging my clit. "Baby, I'm about to come again!" I warned him as my mouth watered and body stiffened. That only gave him motivation to go harder. He rammed inside me hitting my spot sending me over the edge again.

"Shit," he pulled out as I exploded. I felt his warm wet mouth on my pussy sucking every drop he could into his mouth. Once he was satisfied with my taste, he drove his dick inside me again. I started throwing my ass at him, causing him to groan loudly. "That's it baby, throw that pussy on me." He spanked my ass knowing how much that turned me on. I reached down and tugged on his nut sack knowing that was his weakness.

"Fuuuuccckkk!" he roared as he dug his nails into my ass. I pulled away from him and turned around. I swallowed his entire dick in my mouth. I slurped and sucked until he released his thick milk down my throat. His body jerked and shook until I was sure I vacuumed every drop from him. We both collapsed on the bed trying to regulate our breathing.

"I need to go away more often, if I get to come home to this," I said cuddling up next to him.

"You can get this whenever you want, if you move your ass in with me Tawny," he said smacking me on the ass.

I giggled. "I've been thinking about it a lot lately. We both are so busy, we don't get to see each other. I miss this. I miss you Ry."

"You know I love your ass. I'm just waiting on you to say you ready to move in," he said sitting up resting his back on the head board.

I sat up and looked him in the face. I knew he was serious. He has been trying to get me to move in with him for the past few months. I'm so worried about giving up my independence and freedom. I don't mean freedom to date anyone else. Riley was it for me. He was the one I wanted to build a life with. I just like coming and going without having to inform anyone. I had so many more goals I wanted to accomplish before settling down. I know the type of man Riley is, my role as his girlfriend will change to the role of his "wife." I know with that status he's going to want certain things from me that I'm not ready for.

"Can I make a decision after our vacation next weekend?" I asked with a smile.

"We've been doing this shit for a while now Tawny. All this good fucking with no growth in our relationship is pointless," he said. That was one of things I absolutely loved about Riley, he always expressed how he felt. He wasn't one of those men that felt like telling a woman how he felt made him weak. He was that sure of his manhood and I loved it.

"So, no more fucking until I make a decision?" I asked with a smile straddling his lap.

"Hell no, I'm going to fuck a decision out of you," he said rolling me on my back. The remainder of the night was us in the bedroom making up for time that we've missed together.

It was Monday morning, and I didn't open the studio on Mondays. I woke up and cooked Riley a big breakfast before he left my apartment. I was going to get my hair braided, then relax at the spa for a few hours. We had a great time in Reno. Jiera and I were shocked to see Max show up that night. One minute him and Lexi can't stand each other, the next minute they can't get enough of each other. I can't help but smile at them when they are happy together. It's obvious they love each other, but it's toxic at the same time.

After cleaning up the kitchen, I took a long, hot shower. I was still sore from the workout Riley gave me last night. Just the thought of him sent chills down my spine. I slipped on a pair of light blue distressed jeans, an off the shoulder, long sleeve red top and a pair of black pumps. After getting my hair done, I decided to hit up the mall before going to the spa. I wanted to find a couple of dinner dresses to take with me for our vacation. I loved going to the mall on Mondays, because it wasn't overcrowded. The weather was perfect in October, not too cold or hot. Once I entered the mall, I went straight to Neiman Marcus. I didn't take long to find a couple of sexy but classy dresses. I ended up buying a couple of pair of stilettos that I didn't need, but they were too pretty to resist. I headed to the food court to grab a bite to eat before leaving.

I was sitting down eating my bourbon chicken when I heard a familiar voice approaching me. I hadn't heard his voice in over a year. I looked up and stared into the eyes of the man that I once loved with all my heart. Tone was himself again. He had picked his weight back up. His body was more chiseled than I remembered, and his skin looked as if it was dipped in milk chocolate. He still had his beautiful dreads that hung to his shoulders. I had to take a minute to take him in.

"Hi," I said looking up at him.

"What's up Tawny?" He asked showing his pearly whites.

"Just enjoying my day off," I said.

"Damn, it's good to see you. It's been a while," he said. "Can I sit for a minute?"

I was hesitant about having him sit with me. I don't know why I felt like I was doing something wrong. I knew Riley wouldn't like this if he walked up on me sitting down with my ex-boyfriend, that tried to destroy his best friend and killed his baby. I know all that was the past, but I know they still held some animosity toward Tone. I know that man that did those things wasn't the man that raised his sister, and showed me love like no one had ever given me until Riley came along.

"Sure, I don't mind," I said gesturing for him to sit down.

"How have you been?" He asked staring at me.

"I'm good. I have no complaints," I said with a smile. I don't know why I was nervous sitting here with him. It was like he was making me blush without even trying. It was the way he was looking at me. It made me think of the way he once looked at me.

"Congratulations on your studio...for real this time," I said with a smile.

"Thank you," I said with a head nod.

"I apologize for ruining your opening night. I know how hard you worked to make that happen. There's so many things I'm sorry about Tawny," he said with sincere eyes.

"It's in the past. We've all moved on," I said refusing to look him directly in the eyes.

"Thank you. I wanted to reach out to you and apologize so many times, but I didn't think you wanted to hear it," he said.

"It's okay, really Tone. How's Minnesota treating you?" I asked wanting to change the subject.

"I hated it at first, but now it's home. It's where I want to be. I just wish my daughter was there with me," he said.

I noticed he didn't include Toya in that statement. I chose not to speak on it. It was no concern of mine. "She's beautiful Tone."

"Thank you. She's a reminder that I did something right in this world."

"You did a lot of great things Tone. Look at Jiera. She's a boss lady now. You are responsible for raising her after your parents died," I reminded him.

He nodded his head graciously agreeing with me. "How's your foster mom. That mean ass woman still kicking?"

I couldn't help but laugh. She hated Tone. She even hates Max. The thing with Ms. Daisy is she hates all men. She feels like the world would be perfect if men didn't exist. It made me wonder if she ever had sex. As nerve wrecking as men can be, I need my man on this earth with me. "Yes, she's still the same old grouchy lady." He laughed and shook his head.

"Does Jiera know you are here?" I asked. I can't believe she didn't tell me Tone was coming home.

"Yea, she told me she went out of town with you. She was supposed to come by yesterday, but was too tired. I'm headed to the store to see her now," he said with a smile.

"Yea, I should get going too. I have a much-needed spa date," I said as I started getting my things together.

We both stood up at the same time. He stared at me and it felt like an eternity. "It was good seeing you Tawny. You are still just as sexy as I remember that day you came walking past our house."

I laughed. "And you tripped and fell trying to catch up with me."

"I told you I did that on purpose," he said laughing.

"Yea, I remember you saying…you got me falling in love with you already. Corny ass line," I said laughing.

"Whatever, it worked," he said laughing with me.

"I better get going before I'm late and they cancel my appointment," I told him.

I gathered my bags and said goodbye. For some reason it didn't feel like a goodbye.

Lexi

"Why the fuck you keep going to that job if you don't like it?" Max asked as he lay in his bed as I put on my clothes. Since the incident at King's house, it seemed as if we were on the right track. I wasn't fooling myself though. Whenever it seems we are making progress, he will shut down. I'm just patiently waiting until the next time.

"It's not that I dislike the job. I love helping and talking with the residents. It's just not what I want to do with my life. I love doing makeup," I said.

"Well do that shit and stop letting your father dictate how you live your life, Lexi. You are a grown ass woman now. Stop trying to seek his approval," he said.

"What if I do it and I fail. He will only rub it in my face."

"At lease you can say you tried. It's better than not trying at all. You won't fucking fail anyway," he said. This is the Max that I love so much, the one that uplifts and encourages me.

I smiled. "I'll think about it."

"Speaking of old people, Granny asked about you the other day," he said. I loved his Granny, Ms. Violet reminded me so much of my deceased grandmother. She was my heart. She was the one that gave me the attention that I couldn't get from my father.

"I'll go by tomorrow. What's your plans for the day?" I asked.

"Scoop my lil princess up and spoil her. You wanna hang?" He asked getting out the bed. Max was tall with just the right amount of muscles that I loved. He wasn't too brawny, but his medium frame was carved perfectly. He had so many tattoos on his chest, abdomen and back you couldn't see his skin.

"You know your baby mama don't like me around her child," I reminded him.

"Fuck her, she's my daughter too and you've done nothing to make her feel that way," he said.

I smiled. "Yes, I did. I fucked with you."

"Nah, you fell in love with me," he said pulling me toward him by my waist. While I placed kisses on her neck, she agreed to spend the day with us Saturday.

"Yea, we can do that. Don't let me have to come to your job and fuck that cornball up," he said staring at me.

I giggled. "Jealous."

"Nah, territorial," he said with a straight face.

"So, I'm yours. Are you mine Maxwell?"

"Always will be," he said before softly kissing my lips.

"Don't start. I have to go home and get ready for work," I said trying to pull out of his hold on me.

"Let me send you to work feeling like you're floating," he said as he started pulling my panties down. I couldn't resist him, and I didn't want to.

He lifted me up by my ass and I wrapped my legs around his waist. He laid my body down across the bed, pulled me to the edge and spread my legs apart. "Sweetest watermelon I've ever had," he moaned as he twirled his tongue like a tornado.

"Ooooh shiittt!" I screamed when his slid his long-wet tongue inside my tunnel, while massaging my swollen clit with is thumb. "Fuck Maxwell, I'm bout to come!"

"Hhhmmm," he moaned as his head twirled, while his tongue licked and slurped all over my pussy. "Come for me Lexi," he moaned right before I exploded causing my cream to splatter all over his face. "Damn, I love the way you taste." He didn't stop until he was bringing me to another uncontrollable orgasm.

I laid there feeling comatose. "Now you can get ready for work," he said looking down at me with a smile.

He looked so damn sexy as I stared at him with my drunken eyes. His long, thick, veiny dick was staring right back at me. My mouth watered at the taste of his sweetness going down my throat. I slowly pulled myself up sitting on the edge of the bed. I wrapped my small hands around his dick and lapped my tongue across the crown. I could feel it jump in my hand as he grunted in his throat. I stroked up and down his dick while my mouth followed along. "Damn!" he barked as I continued to suck him in and out my mouth.

I pulled him out my mouth and started stroking my tongue up and down his shaft. "Fuck, this shit feels good!" He groaned as I reached down and fondled his balls as I went back to slurping and sucking his thick dick in and out my mouth.

"Shit Lexi, I'm bout to bust this shit!" I sucked and moaned on his dick until he was exploding in my mouth. "Aaaaarrrrrggghhh, I fucking love you!" It was rare that Max said those words to me, but I loved hearing them anytime.

After taking a shower, I dressed and headed home to get dressed for work. I was going to be late today. I haven't seen Randall since the night of the dinner party. I know I needed to apologize to him for me and Max's behavior. I decided I would make it my priority to give him that apology today.

Tone

"I'm sorry I didn't make it over last night," Jiera said as I walked into her store.

"It's cool. I had some catching up to do anyway," I informed her. She smiled.

"Boy, I don't want to hear about you and Toya sex life," she said turning up her nose.

I chuckled. "How was Reno?"

"It was fun," she said smiling.

"I just saw Tawny at the mall. Damn, she's looking better than I remembered," I said as a flashback of Tawny's chocolate sexiness flooded my head.

"She's doing great Tone," Jiera stated. I know her statement was her way of telling me to stay out of her life. I had no plans of disrupting Tawny's life, but if I thought I had any chance of having her in my life, I wouldn't pass up the opportunity.

"I'm not trying to get back with her. I just happened to run into her. I had the chance to apologize for all the hurt I caused her. Damn Jay, have some trust in your brother," I told her.

"I'm sorry. You are doing so good. I just don't want you to do anything to disrupt your progress," she said with sincerity.

"I won't. I'm here working on a job. I'll be here for a while. I needed this time to spend with my daughter anyway," I said.

"She's growing so fast," she said with a big smile.

"How's my little nephew?" I asked.

"Chunky and bad," she said with a laugh. "You guys should come over for dinner."

I laughed. "I don't think your husband would like that. I know the only reason I'm breathing is because of you. Let's just set a playdate for the kids at a park or something."

"He's your brother," she said.

"Only by blood Jay. I can't blame the man for having beef with me."

"We'll set the play date, but I'm still going to talk to him," she said. I knew not to argue with her about it. She's going to do what she wants to do. I agreed to the play date and left the rest alone.

"Where's Toya?" I asked her as I looked around the store for her. I wanted to surprise her and take her to lunch.

"She's off today," Jiera said as we walked to the back of the store. The statement threw me off, because Toya told me last night she was working until five o'clock. I decided not to comment on her statement.

"How are things between you and her?"

I shrugged my shoulders. I knew Jiera wanted me to settle down. I could tell she still worried about me. "We good. She wants me to move back, but that's not happening."

"Especially since you are a business owner."

"I like my life now, Jay. For the first time in a long time, I'm living right. That shit had me fucked up. There's a lot of bad memories that still fuck with me," I confided in her.

"You know I already forgave you, don't you?" She asked with soft eyes.

"I know Jay and I love you for that. I'm still coping with forgiving myself. I don't need the negative memories haunting me every day."

"I understand, but you also have to face them Tone."

"That's why I was happy we got the bid for this job."

"Can I ask you something?" She asked. I nodded my head yes. "When did it start…the drug abuse?"

I shook my head. "Hustling and sampling the product. Life was hard as fuck and it gave me an escape from the fucked-up life I had us in."

She looked at me with wide eyes. "I never thought you were responsible for our struggles. I loved and respected you so much for being there for me. You could've taken the easy way out and just looked out for yourself. Don't ever feel like you didn't do enough for me, you did everything for me."

"Yea and look at you now. I'm proud of you Jay," I said with a smile.

A big grin appeared on her face. "Thank you."

"You remember going to Salvation Army shopping for Christmas clothes to wear back to school?" I asked laughing.

"Hell yea, I felt like you were rich taking me shopping."

"Mama would be proud," I said looking at her.

"Yes, she would be," she smiled at me.

"I'm going to get out of here. Hit me up and so we can take the kids to the park or something," I said standing up. I gave her a hug and kiss on the cheek and headed over to Toya's townhouse.

As I was pulling into the driveway behind a car that I didn't recognize. A nigga was opening his passenger side door. I chuckled when Toya exited the car. She stared at me through the windshield with guilty eyes. I can't say I wasn't shocked to see her dating another man. I guess I shouldn't be, since I've been stringing her along.

<u>Riley</u>

"I need you at the damn warehouse ASAP," Max demanded over the phone with urgency. I was making rounds on my businesses and a few spots, before Tawny and I left tomorrow for our trip.

"What's up?" I asked not wanting to drive all the way across town.

"Man, just get here," he said with frustration in his voice.

I knew things had been going too good for us the past year. I had no idea what could possibly be wrong. We weren't beefing with anyone. Product was flowing in and out, just the way we wanted. We hadn't heard anything about us being under investigation thus far. I took a deep breath and made my way toward the warehouse. The warehouse was empty when I arrived. The only car parked there was Max's. I made my way to the small office. He was sitting behind the desk on the phone. I could tell by his expression it wasn't a pleasant conversation.

"Ok, thanks for the info. I'll get back with you in a couple of days," he said ending the call. "Fuck!"

"What the fuck going on?" I asked with concern.

"The entire Santiago family been wiped the fuck out. We gotta find another connect or deal with the Cruz family that is taking over their business," he said.

I flopped down in the chair. There was nothing harder than finding a connect that you vibe with in the drug game. I also felt the loss of the family. They all were good men that we had established a bond with over the past year. "What happened?" I asked.

"Ambushed their asses on a yacht. Entire damn family was on vacation together…children and all," he said shaking his head.

"Did the Cruz family do it?" I asked.

"Nobody knows. The heads of the Cartel made the decision to give it to them," he said.

"Damn," I said shaking my head.

"I don't know shit about them mothafuckas, but talk ain't good," Max told me.

"What talk?" I asked.

"That was Orpheus on the phone. He knows them."

"How long before we need a re-up?" I asked.

"A couple of weeks."

"Let's start looking for a new connect. Damn, I guess I gotta postpone this damn vacation. Tawny's going to flip," I said shaking my head.

"Nah fam, I got this. I'm only going to research. This one of those times we need King. He knows a lot of families," he said. I shook my head in agreement.

I hung with Max discussing the business before I decided to swing by my parent's house. I wanted to see them before I left tomorrow. My dad was sitting in his favorite chair watching sports. I sat in the recliner next to him. "What's up Pops?" I asked.

"Relaxing Junior. What brings you by today?" he asked glancing at me.

"I just wanted to come by and see my two-favorite people before I head out of town tomorrow."

"Where are you going?" My mother asked walking into the den.

"Jamaica with Tawny," I said. I waited for her reaction.

"So, you still dating that stripper?" She asked not trying to hide the disappointment in her face.

"Lillian, don't start that shit. That girl makes him happy let them be," Pops said looking up at Moms.

"I just want my son to marry a respectable, nice, homely girl," she said.

"Yo ass wasn't homely. You even smashed one of my homies," Pops said with a scowl on his face.

Moms pale pink skin turned red. My mother was Latino and Irish. My dad was African American and Caucasian. With all the different races in us, we still were considered black in America. That was perfectly fine with me. I wouldn't have it any other way. Pops knew how to get under Moms' skin. I knew he was only saying those things to shut her up. I had to laugh at his remark.

"Pops what you know about smashing?" I asked with a laugh.

"Shit, ask yo mama...she know," he said winking at her.

"Bring that girl over for dinner. You talk about her, but never bring her here," she said ignoring Pops and looking at me.

"I will when you are willing to forget that she was a stripper," I said.

"Was?" She asked.

"Yea Moms, I told you she opened a dance school," I said with pride.

"Yea sweet cheeks, she teaches strip and pole dancing classes. Go sign up for a couple so I can watch that lil ass jiggle," Pops said reaching over and tapping Moms on the behind. I burst into laughter. She smacked her lips, rolled her eyes and walked out the den

Pops laughed. "Don't pay your mom any mind. If that girl makes you happy that's all that matters. Trust me, your mother wasn't all that innocent." He winked at me and took a swig of his beer.

"Y'all still in love?" I asked.

"Wouldn't trade her nagging ass for nothing in the world. She's a good woman. She just being a protective mother. Bring the young lady around. Let us meet her," he insisted.

"I will, when we get back. Don't be looking at her ass ol' man," I said with a smile.

"Sssshhhit," he said with a smile. I burst into laughter. I chilled with my old man for a couple of hours before heading back out to finish what I was doing before Max interrupted me. I couldn't get my mind off what happened to the Santiago family. That shit touched my heart. They were good people. It made me think about the chances I take with my life every day.

Tawny

"Yea girl, I'll be there. I'm with my foster mom at the doctor's office for her checkup right now. I'll be to the restaurant at eight," I told Jiera over the phone as I sat in the waiting area of the doctor's office.

"Ms. Greene," the nurse called her name. I stood up to follow her to the back.

"Where the hell you going? I don't need you following me back here. I can talk for myself," she said looking up at me.

Ms. Daisy was a mean grouch. She always has been since the day I came to live with her. She was strict and mean raising me. Social services brought me to her when I was ten years old. The school reported my biological parents when I wasn't in school for over three weeks. They never tried to get me back when I was taken away. At ten years old, I was basically taking care of myself anyway. At first, I hated living with Ms. Nancy, but she eventually grew on me. She would never admit it, but she cared about me too. When social services came to take me away to go to another home, she fought to keep me there with her. She didn't have any family.

"I want to hear what the doctor has to say. I want to make sure you are taking your blood pressure medicine like you should," I told her.

"Chile and if I'm not, what the hell are you going to do about it? Sit your ass down and wait until I'm done," she said walking away. I shook my head and sat my ass down like she said.

I sat and scrolled through my social media accounts and emails. I was excited about the new classes already being full. When I return from our vacation, I was going to start looking for a location for my second studio. I'm going to enjoy this time away with Riley. I'm still undecided on moving in with him. There's so much more that I want to accomplish, although I think about focusing on building a life with him. I had to smile when I came to a picture of Tone and his little girl. She was a cutie. It felt good seeing him truly happy again.

About thirty minutes later, Ms. Nancy came walking back into the waiting room with the doctor behind her. She didn't look happy. "Is everything ok?"

"Well, her blood pressure is too high, and she needs to watch her cholesterol. Proper dieting should help. It wouldn't hurt if she lost a few pounds." Ms. Nancy was only about five feet six inches and wore about a size twenty-two. She has a dark skin complexion with salt and pepper hair that she wore back in a bun. Her black rimmed glasses sat on bridge of her nose. She always looked over them when she talked to you. "Just make sure she takes her blood pressure medicine," he said looking at me.

"She's not my damn mama. What are you telling her for?" Ms. Nancy asked looking up at him. He chuckled.

"I'll keep a closer eye on her," I told him.

After leaving the doctor's office, I went to the pharmacy to fill her prescription. I took her to pick up a few groceries then we headed back to her house. My phone rang as I drove. I smiled seeing Riley's name on the screen.

"Hi Ry," I said with a school girl smile on my face.

"Just checking on you baby," he said in his deep sexy voice.

"I'm taking Ms. Daisy home and then I'm headed home to finish packing."

"Hi Ms. Daisy," he said loud enough for her to hear since I had him on speaker phone. He knew she didn't like him. It never bothered him. He would still treat her like she was his favorite person. Sometimes, she acted like she wanted to like him and then she didn't.

"Hi," she replied dryly.

"Where are you?" I asked.

"Just making some rounds before I head your way," he said.

"Okay, I'm going out for drinks later with the girls," I informed him.

"Yea, I got some shit to do anyway," he said.

"Boy watch your damn mouth around your elders," Ms. Nancy said loud enough for him to hear.

"My bad," he said with a laugh.

"I'll talk to you later," I said before we ended our call.

"Your grown ass asking some white boy can you go out. What's wrong with you chile?" She asked staring at me as I drove. "I didn't raise you to depend on no man and damn sure didn't raise you to be submissive to any man."

"I didn't ask him, I informed him. Riley is not white. He's a good man," I said glancing at her.

"Girl, that damn boy just as white as my damn doctor. He probably dating your pretty chocolate ass to make himself feel like he black," she said. I laughed. One thing she always did was compliment me on my deep chocolate skin tone.

"Listen chile, don't let these men control your life. Don't put your all in a man and lose focus on yourself. I did it and ended up alone. I gave up on all my dreams to build a life with him only for him to cheat and leave me for the next woman," she warned me. That's the most she ever shared with me about her life. She only talked about her parents and sister whom are all deceased now.

"Riley isn't like that."

"Ain't none of them like that until it happens. Use them for what they are worth. A good fuck and keep it moving," she said looking straight ahead. I shook my head and didn't reply.

Max

"Thanks for coming baby," Granny said as I walked in the kitchen.

"I'm only doing this for you. I know you love her, because she's your daughter. I don't have any kind of love to give her," I told her.

She nodded her head. "I know it still hurts you Maxwell. I want you to do this for yourself not for her. You need to release that hate you have for your parents to become the man I know you want to be for Lexi."

I didn't have a reply for her comment. I wanted to love Lexi the way she loved me. I wanted to show her I appreciate and cherish her more than she knows, but I didn't know how I can do that when I had so much anger and hate built up inside me.

"Why she wants to see me so bad after all these years? I was locked up for four years and never received a letter, call or visit from her," I asked.

I sat down at the kitchen table next to Granny as she peeled potatoes. "I guess she finally seeing the error of her ways."

"She doesn't treat you any better. She acts like she's ashamed to call you her mother and me her son," I said shaking my head.

"Your mother always wanted to live the glamorous life. I was never able to give her that. She thought she found it with your father, but we both know how that turned out. When the next rich man came along, she saw her opportunity and took it."

"Yea, leaving me behind because she didn't want the baggage," I reminded her.

"Baby, that was her loss," Granny said touching the side of my face.

"She left me in the pits of hell," I said staring at my Granny. I could see the tears forming in her eyes. I didn't have any more to shed over the life I was dealt. I refused to open my heart to allow that kind of pain again.

There was a knock at the door. I knew it was her. I haven't seen the woman who birthed me since the day she left our home when I was eleven years old. I don't know why she was so adamant about seeing me. I'm sure it's something she wants. Whatever it is she damn sure won't get it from me. I remained seated at the kitchen table while Granny went to answer door.

"He's in the kitchen. I'll leave you to talk," I heard Granny say to her.

I could hear her heels clicking against the hardwood floors as she made her way to the kitchen. My only thought was I wonder was the expensive shoes worth losing your only child. I stared her in the eyes the moment she walked in the kitchen. I wanted her to see that I had no feelings toward her. She stood there staring back at me with water in her eyes. I still felt nothing for her. If anything, rage started to creep into my heart.

"Hi," she said softly.

She was still as beautiful as I remember her. She was medium height, slender with an hour glass figure. Her long wavy, black hair was down her back. She has a pointy nose, full lips and eyes as black as midnight. We both had the same light tan skin complexion. I nodded my head at her. She slowly made her way to the kitchen table and sat across from me.

"Wow this house is nice," she said looking around Granny's oversized kitchen. I didn't reply. I knew she wanted me to brag about purchasing the house for my Granny, but I had no desire to impress her.

"I remember our old kitchen. The entire house could probably fit in this kitchen," she said with a slight laugh.

"What do you want?" I asked getting impatient with her small talk.

"Your forgiveness," she said staring at me.

"Fine it's done," I said standing up to leave. I couldn't do this. Staring at her reminded me of all the pain I went through as a young child.

"I know it's not that easy Maxwell. I'm willing to work to get your forgiveness."

I walked over to her and stared down at her. "I cried every night for you to come back. I cried until I couldn't cry any damn more. I decided my life was worthless. I felt worthless. I didn't give a damn about shit in this fucked up world. All this shit I felt is because you wanted all this expensive ass shit you have on. Don't ask for my forgiveness, forgive your damn self. You'll never get it from me." I walked out the room leaving her seating there.

Lexi

"**H**ey Lex, can you drop me off to Sade's apartment. I need to go get this sew in done," Drea said catching up with me as I walked down the hall at the elderly facility.

"Yea, I'm going to get my stuff out the locker and I'll be right out," I told her.

"Ok, I'll just wait outside for you," she said walking away. After retrieving my things, I headed toward the exit. I was surprised to see Randall. I have been looking for him for the last few days at work, but he hasn't been here.

"Randall," I called his name as I sprinted to catch up with him. He was walking down the hall toward the front desk.

He stopped to face me. I could tell by the look in his eyes he was still upset with me about the dinner party. I couldn't blame him. I pulled him into a situation knowing what would happen. This is the kind of petty shit that Max makes me do. I owed Randall an apology for being inconsiderate. "I've been looking for you," I said looking up at him.

"I took a few days off to visit my parents," he answered.

"Oh, is everything okay?"

"Yes," he answered bluntly.

"Randall, I just wanted to apologize for the dinner party. I was wrong for inviting you there knowing my ex would be there. You didn't deserve that," I said with sincerity.

"I thought you were different. Those are the type of people you like to be around, strippers and drug dealers. I could never take someone like you home to my family. I come from a family with morals and class, something you surely know nothing about. Fucking boys in bathrooms, that is so low class. I guess I shouldn't expect any better from a stripper," he ranted.

I stood there and listened before his words started to fade away. I was losing all the control I tried to hold on to. The next thing I remembered was staff members pulling me off him. I made sure to kick him as hard as I could between the legs when I was being pulled away from him. I caught a glimpse of his face and it was bloody from the scratches I made digging my nails into his skin. I was hauled out of the building by security.

"I can't believe I lost my job over that pompous asshole," I said wiping tears as I drove to drop Drea off.

"I can't believe he said all that shit to you. I didn't know you were interested in him," she said staring at me.

"I wasn't at first, but you know how things are with me and Max. I decided maybe I needed to try a different type," I confessed.

"Girl, that nigga ain't shit. He be breaking me off to fuck him in his office. How you think I'm paying for this sew-in?" she asked flashing a few hundred-dollar bills.

My mouth dropped open. "Why didn't you tell me?"

Rebellious: A Rebel Spin-Off Nona Day

"Hell, I didn't know you were interested in him. Chile, you ain't missing nothing with his lil dick ass," she said rolling her eyes. I couldn't help but laugh.

"Maybe they won't fire you. They may just suspend you for a few days," she said trying to make me feel better.

"Drea you know as well as I do I'm good as gone," I said shaking my head.

"I'm sorry Lexi. You are a cool ass chick. I hate this happened to you," she said with sadness.

"Maybe this was meant to happen to push me to do what I really want to do," I said to her.

"Yes bitch, you can practice on my pretty ass face anytime," she said with excitement. I giggled.

"Don't worry, leave Mr. Smalldick to me," she said smiling and nodding her head. I warned her not to do anything to jeopardize her job. He wasn't worth it.

"What the hell is Maxwell doing over here?" I asked we pulled into the parking lot of Sade's apartment building. She glanced at me. "Who is he fucking over here, Drea?"

She shook her head. "Honestly, I don't know. I've never seen one of his cars over here." I sat there fuming as water filled my eyes. I knew Maxwell had no business in this part of town. It had to be some bird he was fucking. "Do you want to know?" My eyes shot to hers. I shook my head yes and I wiped the single tear from my cheek.

"Come on," she said getting out the car. I followed behind her. "Rosco, come here," she yelled toward a group of boys standing outside in front of the apartment buildings.

"What up sexy?" He asked with his eyes roaming our body.

"Boy, yo lil ass still peeing the bed. Stop trying to act grown," she said hitting him upside the head. "Whose apartment Max in?"

He shrugged his shoulders. I could tell he was lying. "Stop lying," she said swung at his head again, but she missed him when he ducked and laughed. "You get paid to stand yo lil ass out here and watch everything."

"I get paid, so if you want info I need to get paid sexy slim," he said with a smile. He had to be no more than thirteen. I could tell he was going to be a fuck boy when he gets older. Drea looked at me and shrugged her shoulders. I went to the car and retrieved twenty dollars. I walked back over and gave him the money.

"Monique," he said walking away.

"Come on, Sade will know which one she stays in. I don't know the bitch," Drea said as I followed behind her.

Once we entered Sade's apartment Drea got the info I wanted. I immediately made my way to the apartment. I banged on the front door with Drea standing behind me. "Stop banging on my damn door like that! I'm coming!" the girl screamed from the other side.

She opened the door with a smirk on her face. "What are you doing here?"

"Where is he?" I asked with an attitude.

"He's sleep," she said with an attitude propping her hand on her hip. She has no idea this is not the day to fuck with me. I pushed her out the way and she pulled me by my arm. I turned around and hit her in the face with my fist. I wanted to scream out in pain. I knew I had broken some bones in fingers. I couldn't tell if the blood was coming from her mouth or nose. I didn't care as I made my way to the bedroom. I guess Max heard the commotion, because she was screaming like she was dying. He came running out the bedroom.

"Fuck Lexi, what you doing here?" He asked staring at me with big eyes looking confused.

"I'm done Maxwell. Please, if you ever cared anything about me, let me go. I don't deserve this, and you know it," I said staring at him fighting the tears from falling.

"This shit ain't nothing Lexi," he said walking toward me.

"You are so right. This shit here between us ain't shit," I said before I turned and walked out the door.

I stormed out of the apartment building. Not only was my heart aching, so was my hand. I looked down at it and it was already swelling. I went straight to the ER.

Tawny

This morning was not the way I wanted to start our vacation and my birthday. Before leaving for the airport, two cars were delivered to my house for my birthday. I purchased myself a 2017 E-Class Mercedes Benz. It was delivered an hour before Riley pulled up driving a 2017 Aston Martin Vanquish, my dream car for my birthday gift. He was pissed that I went and purchased a vehicle without telling him. It's my money, I don't see what the big deal is.

Once we arrived in Jamaica, he seemed to be more relaxed. We unpacked and took a long, hot shower to prepare for our dinner reservations. I wore a backless, strapless black bodycon dress with a pair of gold, open toe red bottoms. I had my hair styled with long Peruvian curly extensions that hung over my shoulders.

"You about ready?" Max asked walking into the room looking edible. He wore a black dinner suit.

I smiled at him. "You look very handsome."

He smiled. "You know I gotta love you. I hate dressing like this."

I laughed. "I know."

"Come here," he said staring at me. I walked over to him and he took my hand. I followed him to the suites' living area. He picked up a beautifully wrapped Tiffany box off the small table. I smiled and reached for it. "Or have you purchased yourself some jewelry too?"

I gently shoved him and laughed. "No, I did not."

"Happy Birthday T. Thank you for blessing me with your love over the past year," he said giving me the box.

I couldn't help, but get emotional. When I first got involved with Riley my head and heart was screwed up over Tone. I was only dating Riley to get over the hurt Tone was causing me. I never imagined Riley would be the man that he is. He's masculine in every since of a man, but also has a gentle, loving side to him that melts my heart. Not a day goes by that he doesn't call to check on me and tell me he loves me. He tends to my needs and wants whenever I've had a bad day. I fell in love with him with no plans of ever stopping.

"You're going to make me ruin my makeup," I said fanning my face to dry my eyes. I chuckled. I opened the box to find a beautiful Pandora bracelet. He had a crown, stiletto and ballerina shoe on it already.

"The crown is for my queen; the stiletto is for your sexiness and the shoe is for your dancing. I'll be sure to have a new charm every special occasion we have together," he said with a wink.

I threw my arms around him holding him tight as I could. "I'm sorry about the car. I'm going to return it when we get home. I want the one you purchased anyway."

He laughed. "I was taking it back any damn way. Let me provide for you the way I want Tawny. You don't have to do shit alone anymore. That's what I'm here for." I shook my head in agreement.

We ate the most delicious food and drank expensive wine. After leaving the restaurant, we went to a night club. I was totally wasted. Riley sat and watched me dance on the dance floor by myself. I made sure to entertain him. I swayed my body touching myself seductively while Ro James' Permission played over the club. He took as much as he could take before he pulled me off the dance floor leading me out of the club.

He sat across from me gently gripping my knees and spreading my legs apart inside the limo. He stared into my eyes licking his lips. "No amount of food on this earth can satisfy this hunger I have right now." My juices spilled into my lace thong, as my mouth slightly opened to exhale the breath that was stuck in my throat. He kneeled between my legs and started placing soft, wet kisses on my thighs as he removed my thong. My skin started to become clammy from the sweat that he was causing to escape my pores. Soft and hard bites on my inner thighs caused me to soak the soft leather beneath me. *Sllluurrrppp.* The sound echoed through the limo as he sucked my drenched pussy lips into his mouth separating them with his tongue. Long, wet strokes from his tongue caused me to twirl my hips to feed him every drop from my essence. "Mmmmm," he moaned as he twirled his tongue inside my lips licking and sucking, as I continued to leak like a running faucet.

"Ooooohhh Ry! Baby, that feels so good!" I whimpered as water started to fill my mouth. He slid two fingers inside me, causing my entire body to quiver as I gripped the back of his head. He pushed my knees up to my chest and slid his tongue down the middle of my ass cheeks. "Oooooohhhh yyyyessss!" I screamed out unable to control myself from the sensations he was giving my body.

"You taste so damn good," he murmured before sucking on my swollen, throbbing clit.

"Ry baby, I'm bout to come hard as fuck!" I moaned feeling myself getting ready to explode. A loud grunt escaped his mouth, as he turned into a mad man to satisfy his hunger. Unable to hold it any longer I exploded squirting my fluids all over his face. I shivered and convulsed as he licked and slurped all he could. He lifted his head with my juices dripping from his low-cut beard. I leaned forward conquering his mouth to taste myself mixed with the sweetness of his tongue.

He lifted me up as he sat back in the seat. I straddled his lap as he pulled my dress over my head. I threw my head back as I enjoyed the much-needed attention he was giving my breast. I was grinding on the huge bulge in his pants, as he flicked his tongue over my hard nipples while massaging them. I wrestled with his pants, until I unleashed his rock hard thick dick. Gripping it with one hand I lifted it and placed it at my entrance. Before I could make a move, Riley grabbed me by my waist slamming me down on his dick. "Aaaahhhh!" I moaned from the feel of his thickness spreading my soaked tunnel open.

"Ride this dick for me baby," I moaned as he guided my body up and down his pole, splattering my juices over us. "Damn this pussy feels better than it tastes!" I planted the soles of my feet into the seat and squeezed my walls around his dick pouncing up, and twirling my hips on every down stroke. "Ssssshhhhit!" He groaned slapping my ass, which only turned me on more. I started rocking back and forth as he gripped and massaged my ass cheeks.

I gripped his face between my hands. I wanted to stare at him while he unloaded inside me. My mouth was wide open as Riley continued to hit my g-spot bringing me to the edge. Our eyes were locked on each other with neither of us able to say a word. We were so lost in the bliss that we were feeling. My body floated in the air as we both exploded with deafening moans. I collapsed in his arms as we both breathed heavily.

"Your pussy can bring World Peace," he said nibbling on my ear. I burst into laughter.

I sat up and stared at him. "It's not mine, it's yours. It'll always be yours." I love him too much to ever let him go.

Tone

"Jay, you sure it's cool for me to be here?" I asked as we sat in the den of their home. "I don't want to cause any issues in your marriage.

She smiled while she played with my daughter. "Yes, King knows you are here."

"How you make that happen?" I asked holding Mufasa on my lap as he sucked on his bottle.

"We argued because I didn't tell him where I was going with Mufasa the other day. I finally told him, and he said to invite you over here," she said shrugging her shoulders.

"I'm not the fucked up, weak nigga anymore Jay. I'm not going to allow him to disrespect me. I don't give a damn if I am in his house. If he wanted me dead he should've done that shit already," I told her.

"If I wanted you dead, you would be. Keep talking shit I can still make it happen," King said walking into the study.

"Nigga, I'm not going to bitch up for you. Only thing I can do is apologize for the shit I did to you and my sister. That's all I can offer you. Ain't no ass kissing coming from me," I said standing up to face him with his son in my hand.

He laughed. "Look at you, acting like a damn man. Sit yo ass down. I don't expect you to kiss my ass. What I do expect is for you to be the brother your sister loves, and I accept your apology. I have no beef with you unless you want to make some."

I sat back down. "Nah, we good. Just don't hurt my sister."

"Damn, you like some kind of super hero when you sober," he said smiling. I chuckled and shook my head.

"Hey baby," he said leaning down kissing Jiera. She smiled and kissed him back.

"I had to work later than I thought at the store, so dinner will be late," she told him.

"I'll take you out to eat. You don't have to cook. Just feed me desert," he said winking at her. She blushed and giggled.

"We can't go out to eat. Your mother and Tawny out of town. Lexi isn't feeling well right now, thanks to your friend," she said rolling her eyes at King.

"Man, don't start blaming me for that shit. Matter of fact, you stay out of it. You know how those two are," he said sitting down beside her. She pouted and remained quiet. He wrapped his arm around her pulling her closer to him.

"I'll watch him," I said looking at them both. King looked at me as if I was crazy.

"Nah, we'll just order take out." I saw Jiera nudge him in the side.

"Man, I swear my son better come back here, the same way he leaves here." I smiled and nodded my head. A big grin appeared on Jay's face. I guess she felt this was a sign of us letting the past go.

I stayed and chatted with Jay for a little more, until it was time for her to get ready for her dinner date. She packed a bag for Mufasa like he wasn't coming back tomorrow. King was adamant about not letting him stay the night, but Jay has a way of getting her way with him.

When we arrived at Toya's place, she was sitting on the sofa watching a reality show. She rolled her eyes at me when I came through the door. She's still mad, because I didn't overreact about her getting out some nigga's car. How could I, when I had already told her if she wants to find somebody else, she's free to do so. I'm not going to worry myself about holding on to someone who isn't patient enough to wait, until I get my life on track the way I want.

"You can stop with that damn attitude," I said sitting the kids down on the floor. Lucindy ran straight to her mama while Mufasa looked around confused.

"I can't believe King let you bring him here. I thought maybe he still wanted to kill you. I guess not being in the streets has softened him," she said.

"Or maybe he just decided to forgive me, because of his love for my sister," I said walking into the kitchen.

"You didn't cook?" I asked.

"I thought we were going out to eat?" She said.

"We've been out to eat three time in the past five days. The other two we ordered takeout. It'd be nice to get a home cooked meal," I said.

"Let's take a vacation," she said getting off the sofa.

"I'm working Toya. I'm trying to build my finances up. I don't have money to splurge," I told her.

"You can get it, if you want. You know JR will give you anything. They have money to throw away," she said walking up to me.

"You're right. It's their money, not mine or yours. My leaching days are over. You either deal with the working-class man that I am, or continue to hunt for a nigga to give you material things. One thing you need to know, I'm not going to lose any damn sleep over it," I said walking away.

<u>Max</u>

I've been calling Lexi nonstop since the day she caught me at Monica's house. Monica was nobody to me. I knew her from coming to my club. She'd been trying to get me to fuck her for the longest. I declined, because I had no interest in her. She was too damn friendly with her pussy. She caught me at a weak moment after the conversation with my mama. After leaving my Granny's house I went to Riley's bar. I got sloppy drunk and she offered to take me home. The next thing I know, I was laying in her bed with my dick down her throat. Unable to resist her wet mouth, I laid back and let her finish. I sobered up when she tried to ride me without protection. I might do some fucked up shit to Lexi, but I would never risk giving her a disease. I threw her ass off me and went to sleep. I was awakened out of my sleep when I heard her screaming like she was being murdered. I jumped out the bed running toward the living room and looked Lexi dead in the eyes. I saw so much pain in her eyes I couldn't do anything, but stand there and stare at her. I was losing the only woman that ever loved me besides my Granny and Maxi, because I didn't know how to love her. She hasn't been staying at her apartment, so I decided to go by her job.

"Yo Drea," I called out when I walked into the facility. She was leaned over the nurses' station talking to another nurse. She looked at me with a frown on her face.

"You already ugly as shit, don't make faces to make it worse," I said with a smile.

"Fuck you Max," she said turning to walk away.

"Yo hold up. You know I'm just fucking with you. You ain't that ugly. You look like that cute Gremlin," I said.

"Ugh bye," she said in frustration.

"Man, stop being so sensitive. You know you ain't ugly damn," I said laughing.

She rolled her eyes. "What do you want?" She propped her hand on her hip waiting for me to speak.

"Where's Lexi?" I asked looking around.

"She's not here," she said.

"She sick or something?" I asked. Lexi had to be sick to miss work. All the dumb shit I've done, she never let it fuck with her money.

"No, you haven't talked to her since that day she caught you with that bird?" She asked frowning up at me.

"Nah, why?" I asked curiously.

"She got fired the same day for beating up Randall," she said.

"What?" I asked wanting her to repeat what she said.

"She attacked the asshole, because he was being disrespectful. Security had to pull her off him," she informed me. She started telling me everything he said to Lexi.

"Where the corny ass mothafucka?" I asked angrily.

"Nah, let me handle him. Every good turn deserves another. Karma is a bitch," she said with a smile.

"Do that and it'll be something nice coming your way," I told her.

"I'm not doing it for yo hoe ass. I'm doing it for Lexi. She's a sweetheart and didn't deserve to get fired. She also doesn't deserve to get treated like shit by the man she loves, Max," she said staring at me.

I nodded my head. "You're right. I know I'm fucking up."

"Now bye," she said turning to walk away.

"Yo, I'm going to let you handle him inside these walls. He'll learn not to fuck with what's mine on the outside of the walls," I told her. She nodded her head and walked away.

I left mad as hell. I wanted to kill that corny ass nigga. I'm going to make sure I catch him outside of these walls. I know Lexi has got to be stressed out about losing her job. It's not that she loves her job, it's the fact she must deal with hearing her parent's down her. Lexi is so determined to prove herself to them she neglects her own happiness. I try to explain to her that even if she makes them happy, she'll still be miserable because she's not doing what she loves. It's funny how I can tell her how to fix her issues, but I don't know how to fix my own. After leaving the job, I headed over to Granny's house.

"Yo Granny," I called her name when I walked through the door.

"Maxwell, I told you about yelling when you walk in my house," she said as I walked in the den. She was sitting down watching Gunsmoke.

"Sorry. I need a favor," I said sitting on the sofa.

She cut her eyes at me. "What?"

"Call Lexi and tell her to come over. Make up some lame excuse," I said.

"Boy, what you did this time?" She asked shaking her head.

"Just do it for me Granny, please," I pleaded.

She shook her head. "When?"

"Now."

I laughed and picked up her cellphone. She told Lexi she had a doctor's appointment and she was stuck with Maxi. She asked if she could watch her until she gets back. I was relieved when I heard Lexi say she was on her way. I smiled and kissed Granny on the cheek.

"You better start doing right by that girl, Maxwell," she said.

"I am. I promise," I assured her.

"You better park that car in the garage. She's not going to stop if she sees your car," she warned me. I hurried and did what she said. I went back into the house and waited for Lexi. Granny went into the kitchen to make her favorite cake for lying to her. I went to open the door when I heard someone knocking. I was surprised she made it here so quick. I scrunched my face up when I opened the door to see my mama standing there. "What the fuck you doing here?"

"I'm still your mother, Maxwell. Show me some kind of respect," she said.

I laughed. "You lost any chance of getting that years ago."

"This is my mother's house. I know she has no problem with me being here," she said.

"Let her in Maxwell," Granny said walking into the living room.

I moved to the side. "I don't know how you stomach her. She doesn't give a damn about you or me. She left me to die and never gave a damn about you."

"It's a mother's love, baby," Granny said looking at me with her soft brown eyes. Out of respect for my Granny, I walked back into the living room.

"Maxwell, we need to resolve our issues. You can't hate me forever," she said following me into the living room. I sat there scrolling through my phone, choosing to ignore her. Only concerns I had right now was fixing this shit with Lexi and finding a new connect. We had too many people to supply to be without a connect.

I knew it was Lexi knocking at the door this time. Granny went to open the door. I never wanted her to lay eyes on the woman that birthed me. I heard them talking and then Lexi storming into the living room. "How dare you get your Granny to lie for you, Maxwell. That's low even for you."

"I'm sorry baby. I couldn't stand to see him looking so pitiful, plus, he agreed to buy me a new car," Granny said with a smile. I smiled back at her. Even though I never mentioned buying her a car, I was going to buy her one. Anything she wants, she gets.

"I'm leaving. Goodbye Maxwell," Lexi said turning to leave out the living room.

"Maxwell, is this your girlfriend?" Mama asked.

Lexi turned to face her. "I guess you another bird. I didn't know you were into older women," Lexi said with an attitude.

My mama laughed. "I'm his mother sweetie."

"Oh my God, I'm so sorry," Lexi said covering her face with her hands.

"It's okay," My mama said with a laugh.

"You need to leave. I got shit to discuss with Lexi," I told her standing up.

"I would like to get to know my daughter- in- law," she said looking at Lexi with a smile.

I didn't understand how she could act as if she did nothing wrong. "I don't want you to know shit about my life!" I barked at her.

"Maxwell!" Granny said staring at me.

"I'm sorry Granny. I know she's your daughter and you will love her regardless, but I don't have anything to offer her. I don't want her to know a damn thing about me. She didn't give a damn when she walked out of my life, so I don't give a damn about her walking back in," I said to Granny.

"I did what I had to do. He was going to kill me," she said with fake tears in her eyes.

Rage took over my heart and mind. "So, you left me there with the heartless bastard to die for you?" I said with anger walking toward her. I felt someone grab my arm and I jerked away. "Fuck this!" I left Lexi standing there with a confused look on her face with Granny and the woman that birthed me.

Lexi

"I'm so sorry about Maxwell's behavior. He has so much anger inside him," his mother said to me as I stood in the living room confused about what just happened. I knew he didn't have much of a relationship with his mother, but I didn't know he hated her so much. Maxwell never discussed his life before getting locked up. The only part of himself he discussed with me was his Granny, that he has so much love for.

"Audrey, I need some time alone with Lexi," Ms. Violet said to her.

"I think I need to be a part of this conversation," his mother said looking at her.

"I think not," Ms. Violet stated firmly.

"Lexi, it's a pleasure to me you. Maybe we can have lunch sometime. I'm going to be here awhile. By the way, my name is Audrey," she said with a smile. I didn't know how I felt about her at this moment. She seemed to cause too much hurt and anger in Maxwell.

"Sure," was the only thing I could say at the time.

"Great, I'll get your number from Mother and call you to set something up," she said with a big smile. She walked out the house, as if her son didn't just blow up in her face.

"Come into the kitchen with me Chile," Ms. Violet said walking toward the kitchen.

"What just happened?" I asked sitting down at the kitchen table.

"Audrey abandoned Max when he was eleven years old. They lived somewhere in California. When she left home, she never looked back. Growing up, she always wanted the rich, glamorous life. That was something we couldn't offer her. Things really got tight when my husband died. Thanks to my brother, Riley's granddad I was able to make ends meet. When she turned eighteen, she married a rich white man. She seemed to have finally got what she wanted, until he started beating on her. She had Maxwell when she was nineteen. My brother tried to intervene and get her out of the situation, but she wasn't willing to give up the lavish life she was living. A few years later, his drinking and bad investment caused him to lose almost everything. He started taking his frustrations out on her even more. We lost all contact with them. All I know from there is she left Max with that monster. I didn't find Max until he was thirteen years old. He was emotionally and physically damaged," she told me as tears fell from her face.

"I didn't know. I thought you raised him. Maxwell never opens up to me. I always asked him questions about his childhood, but he gets upset," I told her.

"That's why. He never talks about it with me neither. I tell you this because I want you to know Maxwell loves you. The problem with him not treating you the way he wants to is, because he doesn't know how to love himself, in order to love you the way he wants. He has to unleash all that hate he has for his mother, and the pain his father caused him," she said.

My eyes stretched wide. "His father abused him."

She closed her eyes and nodded her head. "Those tattoos that cover his torso, covers the pain he's holding inside." I couldn't stop the tears from falling.

"What do I do?" I asked wiping my tears.

"Baby, I wish I can give you the answer to that question. You must love yourself enough to not let that hate in his heart break you. You also have to be strong enough to endure the pain with him," she said placing her hand on top of mine. "If you are not, love yourself enough to walk away."

Riley

"Oooohhhh Ry, don't stop baby, please, don't stop," Tawny whimpered and moaned as I drilled harder and deeper inside her. It was something about seeing her deep chocolate skin covered in sweat, that drove me damn crazy. Loud grunts escaped my mouth, as I continued to thrust inside her, as I pinned her against the wall inside the elevator. Her sling dress hung to her sweet, sweaty skin. My dick was so hard from wanting to be inside her, after enjoying our last night out in Jamaica, I couldn't wait to get her in the room. Her knees were cuffed in my arms with her legs extended over my shoulder. Her succulent breast bounced up and down as I slammed deep as I could go. I looked down at my brick hard dick sliding in and out her, as her juices spilled down onto the floor.

She massaged and pinched her breast, as her eyelids fluttered, and her eyes rolled to the back of her head. Her mouth fell open, but no sound came out. Her juices showered me like a broken damn, causing my knees to buckle. My toes curled up so tight they started to cramp. Electrifying shock waves raced through my body as it convulsed. "Aaaarrrggghhh! Gggggggrrrr!" I roared as I exploded inside her. We didn't stop there. Once we made it to the room, we tore each other' s clothes off and feasted on each other inside the shower.

I woke up the next morning to an empty bed. I looked over to see Tawny standing outside on the balcony. She was damn breathtaking standing there with the sun beaming down on her perfectly sculptured, deep chocolate body. My adrenaline started to pump, as I thought of entering her from behind out on the balcony. I walked out on the balcony and wrapped my arms around her waist while her back was still to me. She turned to face me with a smile on her face.

"I don't want to leave," she said wrapping her arms around my neck.

"Shit, we don't have to. Let's retire and start a family," I told her. "I'm ready to make you my wife."

Her eyes studied mine. I wanted her to see I was serious about moving and this relationship progressing. "Are you serious?"

"Yea Tee, you know what the fuck I want with you. I don't see the point in wasting time," I told her.

"But I have so much more I want to do, before I start a family. I want to open another studio Ry. I want to focus on my goals first," she said.

"Another studio, damn Tawny we never see each other as it is. I'm thinking about leaving the streets to invest in us and you thinking about investing more in just yourself," I said taking a few steps back to see was she serious.

"It's what I've busted my ass for, and I'm not giving up on what I want for anyone or anything," she stated adamantly.

"You act like building a life with me will stop you from doing that. I've never tried to hinder you from accomplishing your goals," I said getting frustrated with her.

"I know. I just want to be my own woman and focus on myself. I know starting a family will consume a lot of my time. Our relationship will change. I know what kind of man you are Riley and I love it. I'm just not ready to be that woman that stands behind you," she said.

I couldn't believe what the fuck I was hearing. "So, I'm good enough to fuck, but not someone you are willing to share your success with?"

"Ry, that's not what I'm saying. You know how much I love you. There's no one on this earth that I want to build a life with besides you. I'm just asking for time," she said softly.

"Yea whatever," I said walking away.

"Now you are mad, because I want to make my own money and not depend on you. I'm not the type of woman that will ever need or depend on a man to provide for her. I will always make sure I can take care of myself," she said walking behind me.

I turned to face her. "Well, what the fuck are you doing with me. I'm the type of man that wants to take care and provide for his woman. If I can't be that man for you, maybe this shit ain't for us." I turned and left the room. I needed time to figure out what the fuck just happened.

Once we were on the plane, Tawny finally broke the silence between us. "I love you Ry. I don't want to end this perfect vacation like this."

"We good Tee. I love you too," I said. She leaned over and kissed me with her soft, sexy lips. Mad as I was at her right now, I still wanted to fuck some sense into her head.

Max

"What's taking this nigga so long, I don't have all day? I asked as we sat to the warehouse waiting for Orpheus.

He needed a re-up and we were going to discuss options for a new connect. Orpheus knew of a few connects that we may be interested in using. Riley sat quietly scrolling through his phone. I looked down at him as I paced the floor. "What the fuck you sitting there so calm for?"

"What good would it be to stress like you. I'm not going to run my blood pressure up for no reason," he said with a smile.

"You just still high from all the pussy you got over the last few days," he said looking at me.

I chuckled. "I guess you ain't getting any, since Lexi dumped your ass."

"Getting pussy ain't never been a problem of mine," he said flopping down in the seat.

It was quiet for a few minutes. He turned his head and looked at me. "I think I've lost her bro, serious shit."

I couldn't help, but laugh. Max was the type of nigga that didn't tell anyone what was eating him up on the inside. That one statement let me know, just how bad he had it for Lexi. "Man, I'm sitting here pouring my heart out to you, and you laughing?"

"That wasn't close to pouring your heart out, but I feel ya. Max, you gotta open up to her. You can't expect her to understand you and the shit you do, unless she truly knows you. I know the shit you've been through. That's why I'm able to tolerate your annoying ass. She doesn't understand you. She thinks you just don't give a damn about her," I told him.

"Man, I'll do anything for that girl. I just don't wanna discuss all that past shit. That shit made me the savage I am today," he said pounding his chest.

"A savage that's about to lose the one love he can't let go," I said staring at him.

The doors opened to the warehouse and I was surprised to see King walking in with Orpheus. "Man, Jay gone kill your ass. What you doing here?" I asked standing up.

He chuckled. "Just coming through to lend my expertise." Riley laughed. "But I was never here," he said with a smile. We all laughed. We shook hands with Orpheus. I still can't believe he bodied KO. He was a heartless, money hungry beast. He was smart and precise in his dealings and movements.

We sat and discussed the three families that we would considered dealing with. King and Orpheus decided we should use all three until we decide we would be the better fit. Even though Orpheus wasn't a part of empire, we treated him like he was. He was our biggest customer. We all decided to take three separate trips Mexico and Columbia. Max and I took the families in Mexico, while Orpheus was going to Columbia.

We all pulled out our guns when we heard the warehouse doors open. It was Animal walking in. "Man, you almost got your body bloodied." I said as he walked toward us.

"Yo it's some Mexican niggas out there wanting to speak with y'all," he said. We all looked around at each other.

"The building secure?" King asked Animal.

"Locked down," Animal confirmed.

"Search them and then send them in," Riley said.

"I'm headed out the back way. I'm like y'all secret weapon," King said with a smile and walked out. I understood King didn't want his reputation on the line and we respected that. This part of his life was over. We knew if we needed him, no one would expect when he came through. We made sure to keep him in the loop of any changes we made, so he would be aware.

Two young ass dudes walked in behind Animal. I could tell just from looking at them I wasn't going to like either of them. They were tall, slender guys with low haircuts and trimmed beards. I could tell they were both cocky as hell.

"Who the fuck are y'all?" I asked staring at them.

"Your new supplier. I'm Juan and this my older brother Felipé," he said with a smile.

"Yea, but we haven't decided on a new supplier. We'll contact you when we do," Riley said to them both.

They chuckled. "It's not your decision to make. The decision has been made by the families."

"Mothafucka fuck you and your families. We choose who the fuck we want to supply us," I told them.

"We'll be in town for a few days seeing how you run your operation. We'll let you know if anything needs to be changed," the older brother said before they turned and walked away.

"This ain't good. If families come together and say no one else is supplying us. We have no choice, but to deal with them," Orpheus said.

"Never going to happen. Them niggas about to dig deep in all our pockets," Riley said.

We sat around and thought of options. We weren't just street niggas, we were our own cartel. We had connections these fools knew nothing about.

Tawny

"Hi baby, where you at?" I asked Riley over the phone. We came back from our trip three days ago and things have been feeling off between us. I know he was still upset about me not ready to settle down yet.

"Handling business," he said. I could hear music in the back ground with people talking.

"In a bar?" I asked with an attitude.

"I'm wherever the money is at?" He stated.

"I thought we were going to the Halloween party at Max's club," I said.

"I'll meet you there."

"Ry, I'm not going to the party by myself," I told him. I was starting to get agitated with him.

"Well, wait until I get there or scoop Lexi up. I know Jay coming with King," he said.

"Ugh," I said hanging the phone up on him.

I know he was only being vindictive, because I wasn't ready to start investing more into our relationship. I love Riley, but I'm going to do what is best for me. Building a solid foundation to know I'll always have my own comes first. I decided to call Lexi to see if she would go to the party with me. I know she probably wasn't going since her and Max have broken up again. I dialed her number and she answered the phone laughing. After pleading with her for a few minutes, she finally agreed to go with me.

I hurried to get dressed. It was almost midnight and I know the club was over packed. I beat my face and slipped on my sexy dominatrix costume. I smiled as I thought of things I wanted to do to Riley in my costume. It didn't take Lexi long to arrive. She was wearing a sexy nurse's outfit. We arrived at the club to see the line wrapped around the building. We walked to the front of the line and were immediately allowed in. We made our way to the VIP to find Jiera. She was dressed in a sexy Catholic School girl costume. We spoke to King and he left us at the table with Jiera. It didn't take us long before we were lit. I had to lick my lips when I saw Riley coming up to the VIP section. He wore a pair of distressed light blue jeans, fitted black tee shirt and a pair of Lebron sneakers. He walked over and sat next to me.

"I got some ideas in my mind for this costume tonight," he said massaging the inside of my thigh. I blushed as my panties became damp.

"I've missed you," I whispered in his ears.

"Sorry baby, I've been busy. I'll make it up to you tonight," he said sliding in his hand closer to my leaking pussy. He sat, talked and laughed with us for a few minutes before he left our table. On the way to King's table, I saw some bird whisper in his ear. I didn't like the look he gave her. Ms. Daisy words started to ring in my ear.

"Damn, Tone in this bitch looking like a whole damn buffet," Lexi said as Tone approached our table. I couldn't deny how sexy he was looking. I was surprised to see him with a girl that wasn't Toya.

"What's up ladies?" He asked staring at me.

"Hey Tone," Lexi and I spoke at the same time.

"Looking nice Tawny," I smiled and blushed. I glanced over at Riley's table to see him whispering in the same girl's ear. I shook my head knowing everything Ms. Daisy said was true. Tone walked off holding his date's hand.

A few minutes later, I received a text.

Damn, I miss you ~Tone

Lexi

I wasn't in the mood to be at the club, but I didn't want Tawny going alone. I took a long, hot shower and dressed. Since it was a costume party, I decided to dress as a naughty nurse. After beating my face, I was ready to go. I wore my hair straight with a part down the middle. *You have to know when to walk away.* I said the words to myself as I stared at myself in the mirror. I was determined to not let Max continue breaking my heart. I grabbed my red clutch and headed out the door. I drove over to Tawny's house since she lived closer to the club.

I couldn't keep my eyes off Max. I wanted to not care about him. I didn't want to love him, but I did. I know Max has done some fucked up shit to me, but he has also helped me gain confidence in myself. The conversation I had with his Granny still played in my head. I had no idea he had been through so much. To look at him now, he was the life of the party in his own club. He had everybody turned up as he popped bottles and smoked. I decided to enjoy myself. I started taking shots of the vodka King had sent to our table. An hour later, I was enjoying myself. Me, Jiera and Tawny danced and laughed until we were exhausted. We returned to our table and my mood changed instantly. Some random bird was grinding her ass on his lap. Our eyes met, and I couldn't look away. The way his eyes seeped into my heart was captivating. His eyes said he loved me, but his actions spoke other words. I forced myself to look away.

"Hello lovely," a tall, slender, nice looking guy said standing in front of me. He looked Hispanic or something. His accent was very strong.

"Hi," I said looking up and smiling at him.

"May I have a seat?"

"Sure," I said scooting over to let him sit next to me.

He took the seat next to me. I can't say that he didn't intrigue me, but he wasn't Max. Max didn't seem to show any interest in me, so I decided to give the gentleman my attention.

"Lexi, you are playing with fire. You know that nigga unstable," Jiera said looking at Max, as he received a lap dance from a stripper.

"Fuck him, I'm living for me now," I said rolling my eyes.

"That's your man," the guy asked.

"Ex. What's your name?" I asked smiling at him.

"Juan Cruz and yours?" He asked with a smile showing his pearly whites.

"Lexi Bradley."

"It's a pleasure to meet you Lexi," he said staring at me.

He made small talk while I tried to keep my focus on him. It was hard, because my heart kept pulling my eyes in the direction Max. I couldn't believe how cold he was acting toward me. He acted as if I was the one who was caught fucking someone else. He wants to play it that way then that's what we will do. After a couple of more minutes of trying to enjoy myself, I was ready to go home. I wasn't going to stay there and let Max continue to disrespect me. Tawny and Jiera were still having a good time. I didn't want to ruin their fun, so I decided to ask Juan to take me home.

"Do you mind taking me home?" I asked Juan.

"No, I would love to," he said with a smile.

"JR, I'm out of here," I said standing up to leave.

"Are you fucking crazy. You don't know this man," she said looking at Juan from head to toe.

"I'll be fine. I'm just getting a ride home. I'll call you when I get there," I said walking away. We made our way outside the club.

We stood in front of the club waiting on the valet. Once we were in the car, he pulled off and turned down the road next to the club. He slammed on the brakes nearly causing my forehead to hit the dashboard. I looked and gasped for my breath. Max was standing in front of the car dressed like Jason from Friday 13th. He had a damn machete long as his leg in one hand and a big ass gun in the other. Even though he had on a mask, I knew it was him. A woman knows the man she loves without seeing his face. *This fool is crazy!*

He walked over to my side of the car and opened the door. "Get the fuck out!"

There was no way I was going to sit my ass in that car. I wasn't worried about my life. I knew Max would kill Juan without blinking an eye. "You don't have to get out," Juan said as I started to get out.

"I don't want any trouble. I'm sorry," I said getting out the car. Max grabbed me by my upper arm and walked me back to the front of the club and put me in his car.

The moment he got in the car, I started swinging on him. "How fucking dare, you? I'm not your property! Go fuck one of those nasty bitches you were getting your attention from in the club!"

He grabbed by my arms. "Calm yo ass down Lexi. You don't know that nigga. You need attention that bad, you willing to fuck a stranger to get it!"

"Fuck you Maxwell!" I tried getting out the car, but he pulled off before I could open the door.

Max

Lexi hopped out the car the moment I pulled into her apartment complex. I knew she was furious with me. I wasn't going to let her leave the club with a nigga she just met. I've been missing the hell out of her the last few days. Every time I glanced at her, I wanted to bury myself so deep inside her, until she felt my soul. I followed behind her. She tried to slam the door in my face, but I blocked the door from closing. I locked the door behind me. I pulled her into my arms from behind. She smelled so damn good as I inhaled her aroma.

"Let me go Max. I know you don't think I'm fucking you. Get out!" she screamed trying to wrestle out my grip.

"You hate me that much you willing to fuck a complete stranger?" I asked.

She burst into tears. I knew she was angry, but I didn't expect her to become that emotional. "Why can't you love me?" She asked turning to face me wiping her tears.

"Lexi, you know I do. My shit just fucked up. I do the best I can."

"If this is your best Max. I don't want it. I'm tired of hurting. I want someone that makes me feel the way I make them feel. I'm not asking for too much. I know I'm not," she said staring at me with pleading eyes.

"I give you everything you want and need Lexi. How the fuck am I not showing you I love you. I know I fucked up a few times, but you know those bitches ain't shit. Nobody comes before you."

"Listen to yourself Max. You are asking me to be okay with you fucking other girls. In the same breath you tell me to realize my value without seeking attention, but you are making me beg for yours. I don't want anyone's attention but yours."

I had no words for her. I stood there and closed my eyes to gather my thoughts. I saw the pain in her eyes. I couldn't keep doing this to her. She deserved more than I can offer her right now.

"What did he do to you Max?" My eyes flew open and she was walking toward me.

"Let that shit go Lexi," I told her not wanting to discuss it.

"You know my deepest thoughts. I share with you my woes about my father's approval. You encourage and uplift me every day. Let me do that for you. You can't keep that pain and hurt buried in you forever. It's going to eat you alive. It's costing you so much right now. Tell me Max," she pleaded with her beautiful eyes.

I stared at her for a few minutes. "What good would it do to tell you that my mother cared so little for me that she left me there with a man that whooped both our asses daily. How is it going to help me to tell you that he used my body for an ash tray? He tied me to the bed and whooped my ass like I was his slave. That's why I covered my body with tattoos to cover the burns and scars on my back. The nigga tried to make me have sex with some woman while he watched on my twelfth birthday." I closed my eyes to fight the emotions that were tearing through my heart. It was too late. I felt the tear slide down my jaw.

"Max," she said moving closer to me.

I backed away. "You right Lexi. I'm too fucked up to love you the way you deserve." I turned and walked away from my soulmate.

Tone

"What's up Sis?"

"Don't what up sis me. Who was that you were with last night and where is Toya?" Jiera asked with an attitude.

I chuckled. "She's just a friend. Far as Toya, I guess she's doing her own thing."

"You guys broke up?"

"She's pissed with me right now. I love her, Jay, I really do. She wants marriage and I'm not ready. I'm trying to build something for myself first," I explained to her.

She shook her head. "Niggas ain't shit."

"What the fuck you mean. I'm doing the man thing and being honest with her," I said.

"No, you just feel like there's something better out there for you since you got your shit together. That girl loved you when you were an addict without a pot to piss in. Now you have a little something, you realize you need time," she said with anger.

"Man, she wants me to give her marriage and vacations when I can't even get a home cooked meal."

"Like I said, yo black ass got a lil something now and she's not good enough now. Toya hasn't changed. She's been the same person since the day you lied and told her you weren't Tawny's boyfriend anymore. She's always been a little naïve, but she's a good girl that doesn't deserve what you are doing to her," she said walking toward the door.

"And one more thing, don't think you stand a chance with Tawny. Riley will kill your ass for sure this time," she walked out the door leaving me standing there speechless.

I didn't fear Riley. If that nigga leaves a weak spot for me to slide in, I'm taking it. I've been texting Tawny all day trying to get her to meet me for a drink. I knew there was tension between her and Riley. They barely talked to each other at the club. After a few more texts, she agreed to meet me at a lil secluded bar.

I hurried and dressed. I made my way over to the bar we were meeting at. I made sure to get a booth in the far back with dim lights. I spotted her when she walked in the bar. I could tell by her clothes, she had just left her studio. She wore a pair of skin fitting black yoga pants, a red tank top with an unzipped hoodie over it. She spotted me and made her way over to our table.

"I'm glad you came," I said as she sat down.

"This is not a good idea for either of us," she said nervously.

"Then why did you come?" I asked. She shrugged her shoulders. The waitress came and took our drink orders.

"You want something to eat?" I asked looking at the menu.

"No, I can't stay long. I have to get home."

"Everything okay with you and Riley?" I asked not giving a damn. Well, I did care to know if she was okay.

"We're good. You know every relationship has its ups and downs."

"Is he treating you right Tawny?" I asked.

She laughed. "Asks the man who treated me like shit."

I laughed. "I did and that was the worst mistake of my life. You are every man's fantasy. I just realized it too late."

"Are you happy with Toya?"

"Like you said ups and downs," I said with a smile. She smiled.

"Damn, you look so damn good. I tried to forget about you, but I couldn't. I think about all the crazy things I want to do to your body," I said licking my lips. I could feel my dick getting hard at the thought of fucking her to sleep.

"I love him, Tone," she said.

"But it's something that made you come here. Tell me you don't still feel that connection we had," I said staring at her.

"I'll always care about you Tone, but what we had is over. I love him enough not to jeopardize what I have with him."

I nodded my head in agreement. "He's a lucky man. If you ever need me for anything. Even if it's just to talk, I'm here for you. I'm mad it's not me, but it's good to know you have someone that loves you." She smiled.

"You remember that night I was embarrassed to bring you over to the house?" I asked.

"Yea, it was my first time. There were no lights. You had candles lit throughout the house. You made it romantic for me," she said smiling.

"I fell so hard for you. I was one of the lowest niggas on the block and you were one of the most wanted chicks. I never felt like I deserved you," I confessed to her.

"You did, Tone. I remember the way you use to just sit and stare at me. You made me feel like I was a piece of precious art, that only you could appreciate. You listened to my dreams. Other niggas only wanted my fat ass," she said with a smile.

"I wanted that too," I said smiling. She laughed and threw a napkin at me.

"Ms. Daisy hated you," she said laughing.

"Hell yea! She ran me out her yard with a shovel," I said laughing with her. "Does she like him?"

I laughed. "No, she thinks he's a white man with a black girl fetish." I burst into laughter.

I enjoyed sitting and talking with her. I know now it's truly over between us. I think I just needed that closure. I walked her out to the car to say goodbye. We gave each other a goodbye hug that felt like a goodbye this time. I didn't feel the heartache I thought I would feel closing this part of my life.

Riley

Max, Orpheus and I were at the warehouse waiting on Juan and Felipé. They were leaving town today and wanted a meeting with us before they left. They both walked in with two Hispanic dudes. "Afternoon gentlemen," Juan greeted us with his arrogance.

"Let's make this shit quick. I've got moves to make," I said to them.

"No problem. Let us introduce you to the new members of your empire," Felipé said.

"Nah, we're not looking for new partners. We good with what we got," Orpheus told them.

"You fellas seem to think this is a request. It's a demand," Juan said.

"Nigga fuck you and your demands. We ain't adding shit to our team," Max said speaking for the first time since we got there. Nigga was in some deep thoughts.

"What's up Maxwell?" Juan asked smiling at Max. I already knew it was about to be some shit.

"Fuck you nigga," Max said walking up to him.

"You still mad because your girlfriend wanted to taste some real dick?" Juan asked. I just dropped and shook my head.

Max hit him in the throat so fast he never saw it coming. He fell to the ground holding his throat. They pulled their guns and we pulled ours. "We can have a shootout, or you can get your punk ass brother to the ER before he dies," I said staring at them with my gun aimed. One of the dudes picked Juan up off the floor as he squirmed trying to breathe.

"You a dead nigga," Felipé said looking at Max.

"Two late mothafucka. I'm a nigga without a soul. I'm already dead," Max said staring at him. They rushed out the warehouse.

"Man, we don't need that kind of trouble right now. We need a re-up in another week," I told him.

"Fuck them fools. The fuck we look like adding some Mexicans to our team?" He asked angrily.

"You know we got some Latino in us, right?" I asked him. Orpheus laughed.

"We got black blood in us, so we black. Nigga didn't they teach you in elementary school that black fades all colors. We are the conquerors," he said with a serious face. I looked at Orpheus and he shrugged his shoulders to say he agreed with Max. I could only laugh.

"We need a connect," Max said finally being serious.

"Them mothafuckas trying to bleed us dry. I'm not copping from them," I said.

"We need to take this trip to Mexico," Orpheus said. We all agreed to leave in a couple of days.

"I'm outta here. You coming over for dinner. Folks wanna see you," I said looking at Max.

"I'll take a raincheck. Tell them I'll stop by soon," he said. I don't know what happened between him and Lexi, but that nigga been on some other shit.

I was taking Tawny to dinner with me tonight. I've been on some petty shit since our vacation. She fucked my feelings up with that independent shit. I love a strong woman, but I need for her to be comfortable in having a man be a man in her life. I'm not sure if Tawny knows what it means to have a man in her life.

I went by her place to scoop her up. I was shocked when I walked through the door. She was wearing a dress that my mother would wear. "Tawny, what the hell you got on?" I asked laughing.

"You don't like it?" She asked with a disappointed look on her face.

"Yea, for my Mama. That ain't you, Tee," I said as I continued to laugh.

"It's not funny Riley. I realized I don't have any appropriate clothes to meet your parents," she said flopping down on the sofa.

I walked over and sat next to her. "Tee, I've seen you in all kinds of clothes. What are you talking about?"

"They are all tight," she said.

I laughed. "That's because that body is a weapon." She smiled. "Go change. I want them to meet you, not someone you think they want to meet."

"I love you," she said kissing my lips softly. I tapped her on the ass when she stood up.

Everyone was sitting in the den when we arrived at the house. I introduced her to everyone. She had already met Riley's grandmother before. I took her by the hand and led her to the kitchen to meet Mama. "Hey baby, I was starting to worry."

"I had some things to handle," I said giving her a hug.

"You must be Tawny?" Mama said looking at Tawny with a smile.

"Yes ma'am. Thank you for having me over for dinner. I made a pound cake," Tawny said handing her the cake.

"You cook?" Mama asked surprised.

Tawny giggled. "Yes, it was a must that I learn, to live with my foster mother."

"Oh, I didn't know you were a foster child," Mama said looking at Tawny with sadness in her eyes.

"It wasn't bad. She was strict, but made sure I was well taken care of," Tawny assured her.

"Riley said you are an exotic dancer," Mama said. I knew she couldn't resist bringing that up.

"I was. I own a dance studio now. I teach strip, pole and artistic dancing."

"What made you become a stripper?"

"The money was good. I knew I wouldn't be doing it forever. I was ashamed when I first started. Then I realized I have more morals than most politicians."

Mama laughed. "So true."

"It's good to see you are a career oriented woman. I've always been a homemaker. I admire you young girls that are choosing to pursue your careers. Just remember those careers can never replace the warmth of a man," she said with a wink. I chuckled. Tawny nodded her head and cut her eyes at me. I shrugged my shoulders.

"Tawny come in here let me show you some embarrassing pics of Riley," Kiley, one of the twins yelled.

"Excuse me," Tawny said hurrying out of the kitchen.

Mama looked at me. "What?"

"I didn't want to like her, but I do," she said.

"Mama you barely know her."

"All I need to know is she loves my son and she's not crazy. I can tell by the way she looks at you she's smitten," she said smiling.

"Who uses that word?" I said laughing. She laughed with me.

"Be careful though Riley. She's head strong and independent. She wants to be in control of her own life. It's going to take the both of you to compromise," she advised me.

Max

"Yo, you with us?" King asked as we sat in his den talking business.

"Yea, the fuck you mean?" I asked looking at him, Riley and Orpheus.

"You acting like your mind a million miles away," Orpheus said.

"I know what the fuck going on. Orpheus has set up a few meetings in Mexico. We are leaving in a few days. I need to watch my back, because I almost killed that pretty ass Colombian," I said with a smile.

"I'm not sure if you should take this trip with us. They might have a mark on you," King said.

"Us, who is us? King, you are not in the business anymore. Why are you going?" Jiera asked walking in den. King gave her a look and she walked out the room pouting and stomping her feet. The only reason King allowed Jiera to know our business is because he wasn't in it. She knew never to repeat what we discussed with Lexi and Tawny.

We all laughed. "Man, stay home. We got this," Riley told him.

Jay came back in the room a few minutes later. "Here's your son. I'm going out for drinks." She sat Mufasa in King's lap and proceeded to storm out the room.

"Man, calm yo ass down. I'm not going," King told her.

"You ain't?" She asked with a smile looking down at him. We all laughed. She walked back over and took the baby out his lap. "I'm going to take him a bath and put him to bed."

We stayed at King's house a couple more hours. I went to Cherry's house to pick up Maxi. I wanted to spend a couple of days with her before leaving for our trip. I knocked on the door and she answered with an attitude. "You have a key. Why you didn't use it?"

I took the key off my key chain. "Here, I'll start knocking from now on."

"What the fuck is your problem?" She asked folding her hands over her chest.

"Nothing, where my baby girl?"

"She's sleep. She has school tomorrow."

"I'm taking her with me. You can pick her up from school Wednesday," I told her as I walked toward the room.

"Why you just can't stay here?" She asked following behind me.

"That shit dead," I told her as I kept walking.

"I guess that lil yellow bitch got your nose wide open."

I turned to face her. "Why the fuck you always gotta comment on her skin complexion. You that insecure in your own skin that you gotta tear another black woman down?"

"Fuck her! Nigga, I know I look better than her."

"Well, go find a nigga that thinks so," I said opening my daughter's room door.

"I bet when I have a nigga sleeping next to me you won't feel that way."

Rebellious: A Rebel Spin-Off Nona Day

I turned to face her. "I don't give a damn about you fucking or loving another man. I hope you find somebody. I just know I ain't the nigga for you. For as Lexi, the disrespect stops now. Regardless, if I'm with her or not, don't let no slick shit come out your mouth about her again."

I left her standing there. I scooped my baby girl up. I had nothing against Cherry. She just wasn't for me. One thing I could say she was a good mother. She never used Maxi against me. We co-parented well together. I just hope shit didn't change since I wasn't fucking her anymore. Maxi never woke up on the way to my house. I put her in her bed and went into the den.

I started thinking about Lexi, wondering what she was doing. Right now, she usually would be curled up under me playing in my hair talking nonstop. I guess she didn't know how to take the information I gave her about my old man. I still wake up in cold sweats from the nightmares of the abuse he gave me. I felt worthless as a child. I prayed for God to kill, because I would rather be dead than live the life I was living. My own mother never came back once to see or get me. I eventually stopped giving a fuck about life. I turned to the streets at the age of twelve. The final straw for me was when he tried to get me to fuck that broad, while he jacked off. I was twelve and whooped his ass like I was a grown man. I ran down the street to one of my friend's houses. His mom called the cops. I was put in the system for a while. I wouldn't talk to anyone. I was always told never to trust the cops, so I kept my mouth closed. They eventually located my Granny. She didn't hesitate to come to get me.

I was too far gone by then. I hated everyone and life. She never gave up on me. I remember hearing her beg my mother over the phone to come see me. She never did. I got sent to prison for four years at the age of eighteen for drugs.

I was jarred out of my thoughts hearing a noise coming from the back door. I pulled my gun out, but it was too late. Two Mexicans rushed in the living room aiming their guns at me. My only concern was my baby girl sleeping in her room. If it was my time to go, I could accept that. I wasn't going to let them kill my baby.

"Only one of us is going to make it out alive," I said keeping my gun aimed on them.

They laughed. "This is for Juan. Oh, and don't worry about your daughter. We'll make sure she makes a lot of money for us when we sell her. Old men love virgins."

I don't know where this nigga came from, but he was my savior right now. I watched Tone creep through the back door as these two fools kept laughing. He gave me a head nod. I put one hole in the center of one of the dude's head while Tone put one in the back of the other's head. They both fell to the floor. I breathed a sigh of relief. I called the cleanup crew to dispose of the bodies. I realized my mind has been so distracted I wasn't watching my surroundings. No one knew where I rested my head. Most people thought I lived in my condo. I didn't want to go there in case someone was waiting for me.

"Fuck! Man, what you doing here?" I asked thankful that he was.

"I was leaving this female's house. I saw the niggas creeping around your backyard."

"Damn, I thought this was it," I said.

"Yea, you better get the fuck outta here. There might be more," he advised me.

"Yea, let me get my daughter. Man, I owe you for this shit. I didn't know you was a killer," I said looking at him.

He laughed. "The only reason I didn't kill y'all niggas is because my sister loves y'all."

I laughed. "Man, shut the hell up! Let's get the fuck outta here." I decided to take Maxi to Lexi's house before getting a hotel room for the night. I didn't want to chance someone coming to look for me at her place or anyone else I cared about.

Lexi

My heart nearly jumped out my chest from the banging on my door. It was almost midnight. I wasn't expecting company. The only person comes to my condo this time of night is Max, and I haven't talked to him since the day he walked out on me. I tiptoed to the door to look through the peep hole. I was shocked to see Max standing there holding a sleeping Maxi. I immediately opened the door.

"Max, what's wrong?" I asked with worry.

"Can we come in?" He asked.

"Yea, why didn't you use the key?" I asked.

"I didn't know if you had company," he said looking at me.

"No one comes here Max. Take her in the spare bedroom," I told him.

He came back into the living room. "Max, what's going on. Is Cherry okay?"

"Yea, she was at my crib. Some shit went down. I didn't feel safe taking her to my condo. I didn't want to wake Granny. I didn't want Cherry knowing about this."

He walked to the kitchen and grabbed a bottle of Hennessey. He took a swallow and stared at me. "Where the fuck you going this time of night?"

"I was doing a video to post on my YouTube channel," I said.

"Oh." He walked into the living room and flopped down on the sofa.

"Max, are you in danger?"

"Shit, my occupation comes with it," he said shrugging his shoulders.

"Get out Max before it's too late."

He chuckled. "It's been too late. This the life I was dealt. I might as well live it to the fullest."

"You don't have to be the life you were dealt. I understand you were raised in a messed-up situation, but you are worth so much more. You deserve better."

He scooted to the edge of the sofa and stared at me as I sat across from him. "You think I'm worth something, Lexi?"

"Yes, you know I do Max. You mean the world to me," I said with love in my heart and eyes.

I scoffed. "If that's true why you never took me to meet your parents?"

"What?" I asked caught off guard by his question.

"It's all good. I understand a nigga like me ain't worthy of meeting a man like your father," he said standing up.

"Max, that's not true! I never felt that way," I explained.

"Listen, I'll come pick her up for school in the morning. I put her things in the room," he said walking toward the door.

"Max stay please," I pleaded.

He walked to me and kissed me on the forehead. "Never doubt what I feel for you Lexi." Again, he walked out my door leaving me speechless.

The next morning, I woke up and got Maxi ready for school. We were sitting at the table eating breakfast while she talked. "Are you going to marry my daddy?"

I smiled. "Do you want me to?"

She shook her head yes. "He loves you. He told me so. Do you love him?"

"Yes. Yes, I do Maxi," I confessed with my heart wide open. A big grin appeared on her face as Max came walking in the front door.

"Hey daddy guess what?"

"What pretty girl?" Max said walking into the kitchen.

"I told you Ms. Lexi loves you too. She just said it."

The look in his eyes as he stared at me was breathtaking. I smiled and dropped my head. "You want some breakfast?" I asked getting up to clear the dishes.

"Nah, I gotta get her to school. Thanks though. Go get your things, Maxi," he said to her. She went running to the room.

"Riley told me you are working with Tawny teaches classes. How's that going?"

"I like it. It doesn't pay what I was making at the nursing facility, but I like the job more," I told him.

"Good, this should help cover your bills for a few months. Fuck what everybody else says Lexi, follow your dreams," he said placing a stack of money on the table.

"Max, you don't have to do that. I have some money saved up."

"I know you do," he said with a smile. "Where you are going early this morning?"

I smiled. "Shopping since I got this stack." We both laughed. "Just kidding. I'm going to let Asia put some plaits in my hair."

"Ok, tell Ariel I said hi," he said walking into the living room. I laughed.

"Are you bringing her back tonight?" I asked hoping he would.

"Nah, I'm taking her to Granny's," he said as Maxi came running back in the living room.

"I don't mind. I like the company," I told him.

"If you sure it's okay, yea I'll bring her back later," he said. I smiled and Maxi high-fived me. He laughed and shook his head.

Tawny

"Hurry up," Jiera said rushing me to close the studio. We were going over to Lexi's condo to hang out for a little while. She was babysitting Maxi. I knew something was going on with the guys, but they weren't talking.

"I'm coming," I said locking up my office.

"I invited Angela to join us," she said as we made our way out to our cars.

"That's good. I can use some of her advice. Fooling with Ms. Daisy, I'm going to turn out a man eater," Tawny said shaking her head.

I laughed. "I follow you."

When we arrived at Lexi's condo. Her and Maxi were baking cookies. Lexi loved that little girl like she was were own. I hope her, and Max can find their way. I know how much they love each other, but I also understand it takes more than love to make a relationship work.

We were sipping and chatting when Ms. Angela, King's mother arrived. She is a beautiful woman that carries herself with class and dignity. Her presence demands attention without her speaking a word. We were having a conversation about finances and our businesses when Lexi noticed Maxi yawning.

"Let me give her a bath and put her to bed. Don't y'all leave?"

"Let me do it. I haven't spoiled this little princess in a while," Angela said winking at Maxi. She giggled.

"Ok, if you don't mind," Lexi said sitting back down. Maxi led Angela upstairs to her bedroom.

We continued our conversation until Jiera changed the subject. "So, you and Max working it out?"

Lexi shook her head no with sad eyes. "He doesn't want me like that anymore."

"Lexi, you know that's not true," I assured her.

"Well, why doesn't he try to touch me? He brought Maxi over at almost midnight and then he left."

"Maybe he's trying to do things the right way this time. He has been acting strange lately," Jiera said.

I laughed. "That's nothing new. He's crazy as fuck."

"Don't say that. He's dealing with a lot. I had no idea is childhood was so damaged," Lexi said with tears in her eyes.

"What happened to him?" Jiera asked stroking Lexi's back.

"What's wrong Lexi?" Angela asked coming back into the living room.

"She's dealing with a lot with Max," I told her.

"He thinks I don't think he's good enough. That's not true. If I had known his childhood was so messed up, I would've been there more for him. He never told me all the bad things that happened to him."

"Yes, he's been through a lot," Angela said looking at Lexi.

"I'm lost," Jiera added looking confused as me.

Lexi went on to tell us what she has found out about Max in the past weeks. I was dumbfounded. It explained why he had a death wish. He didn't think of consequences.

"I can't believe that bitch showed up acting like she did nothing wrong," Angela said with anger.

"I think her returning brings back a lot of bad memories for him. He has so much hurt inside him," Lexi said.

"But he's always been the one to push you to know your worth, but he doesn't treat you that way," Jiera said.

"Because he doesn't know how. He was never shown love, so he doesn't know how to give it the way he wants. Lexi, you were loving the way he empowered you, you forgot to get to know and empower him," Angela.

"I didn't know he needed it. I promise I would have if I had known. I don't know how to get him to talk to me. He just shuts down," Lexi told her.

"Tell him what you see in him. Let him know how strong he is for overcoming what he went through," she told Lexi. Lexi nodded her head in agreement.

"His mother keeps asking to have dinner and drinks with me. I don't feel comfortable meeting her knowing how Max feels about her," Lexi said. "At the same time, I want to know why she did what she did."

"Let that be Max's decision," I told her.

"I agree," Angela said nodding her head.

We all jumped when we heard banging at Lexi's front door. "Jesus, does he have to knock so hard?" Lexi asked herself as she got up to open the door.

She looked through the peephole and turned to face us. "It's not Max, it's Riley and he doesn't look happy."

I immediately stood up and walked toward the door worried about what has happened. Lexi opened the door. My heart started to pound as I stared at Riley. Whatever it was, it was obvious his anger was toward me. He walked into the house and stared me in the eyes. "You fucking that nigga?"

"What? What are you talking about Riley?" I asked confused.

He held his phone up showing me a pic of me and Tone hugging in a parking lot. My heart dropped knowing this wouldn't be easy to explain. I never told him I was meeting Tone for drinks.

"I-it's not what it looks like Riley. I promise," I pleaded with him.

"This the mothafuckin' reason you can't commit to me? You still hung up on this nigga?"

"No, it's nothing like that," I said as I stared into his cold eyes.

"I'm going to let you have that nigga after I whoop his ass," he said staring at me.

"Riley," I heard Jiera say behind me. He turned and walked out the door.

<u>T</u>one

"Ooooohhh yyyeeesss! Right there baby!" Toya screamed as I hammered inside her dripping tunnel. I had her bent over the sofa plowing as deep as I could inside her. I watched my cream covered dick slide in and out of her as she moaned and wailed. I smacked her fat ass to watch it jiggle. She dug her fingernails into the back of the sofa trying to take all she could.

"Damn, this pussy feels good!" I barked giving her ass another smack. I gripped her waist and started slamming my dick inside like I was digging for gold. She started coming so hard I could feel it running down my thighs.

"Oh God! What you doing to me?" She whimpered as her body quivered. I pulled out and buried my face inside her cream covered pussy. Slurping and smacking sounds echoed through the room. Her taste was sweet like icing. I slid my sharp tongue inside her tight hole fucking her with it while I stroked her clit.

"Tooonnneeee!" She moaned my name trying to run from the pleasure I was giving her. I held her still and pleasured her clit making circular motions with my tongue. I nibbled, licked and sucked on it while she screamed out in ecstasy. I didn't stop until she was glazing my face with her icing. After I was done licking her clean, I slid my aching dick back inside her. She spread her legs and arched her back deeper to give me an all access pass.

"Yes baby! This is always yours!" She moaned as I felt my nut building up. I started ramming inside her deeper and harder until I couldn't hold it anymore.

"Shhhiiittt! Aaaarrrrgggghh!" I roared as I unloaded deep inside her.

I flopped down on the sofa next to her. She straddled my lap. "I love you, Tone."

"Stop tripping about bullshit, Toya. That picture ain't shit, but a closure and a goodbye hug. I'm not gone lie, I was feeling something after seeing her after all this time. I realized what we had was history. I love yo ass, but we both need to work on ourselves to make this work," I told her. She nodded her head with a smile.

Someone had sent her a pic of me and Tawny hugging. She went ballistic on my ass. I had never seen that side of Toya before. She's usually timid and calm. I laughed at how seeing her lose it turned me on. The more she cussed my ass out, telling me how she felt about the way I was treating her, the harder my dick got. Before I knew it, I was tearing her clothes off.

"Come on, let's go hop in the shower," I said tapping her on the ass. She giggled and stood up.

After going another round in the shower, we slipped on some clothes to cook a late dinner. I slipped on a pair of jeans and started going over the paperwork from the job we were doing. My uncle taught me a lot about running the business before he passed. I was honored and blessed that he left his business with me. There was no way I was going to disappoint him or my aunt. There was a banging at the door like the police was trying to break it down. I went and retrieved my gun from the safe. I keep it locked up because of Lucindy even though she was with Toya's sister tonight.

"Go in the back. If you hear a commotion, haul ass out the back door," I told Toya. She turned the stove off and went toward the back.

I looked through the peep hole to see King standing there. I breathed a sigh of relief and opened the door. "What the fuck you banging on the door for?"

"Making sure your ass wasn't in here dead," he said walking in.

"What's up?" I asked.

"Riley looking for yo ass. I don't know why and don't wanna know. Jiera came home demanding I come see what's up. Riley ain't the nigga that loses his temper easily. When he does you don't wanna be the one he's mad at," he warned me.

"Ain't shit going on with me and her. If he comes for me, I'm not punking out. I don't give a damn who he is," I said.

"Just watch out for him. I'm staying out of this one," he said looking around. He looked down at the papers spread out over the table. "I see you handling business."

"Yea, something like that," I said.

"Let yo girl help organize this shit for you. All this needs to be in a system," he said.

"Thanks for the advance and the job," I said looking at him.

I chuckled. "Keep up the good work." I wasn't stupid. I knew King had got me the job here. I was grateful, because it was a big contract.

After King left, Toya came from the back. "I'll be back," I told Toya walking in the bedroom to put on a shirt and shoes.

"Tone just stay here. It's only going to be trouble if you go looking for him," she pleaded following me into bedroom.

"I'm not going to be looking over my shoulder for a nigga to come for me," I said pulling my shirt over my head.

"Tone please," she pleaded.

"I'll be back. Lock up," I said before kissing her on the forehead and walking out the door.

<u>Riley</u>

"I heard you were looking for me?" Tone asked approaching me in the strip club.

I scoffed. "Nigga if I wanted to find you, I would've."

"Listen man if you want to handle this shit between us, we can. I'm not going to be looking over my shoulder," he said.

"I'm not the kind of man that kills you from behind. I'm going to look you in the eyes," I said staring at him.

"You ready for that private room, Daddy?" the thick stripper asked straddling my lap.

"Man, you fucking up," Tone said looking down at me shaking his head.

"Mothafucka, did I ask your opinion?" I asked standing up causing the stripper to fall to the floor.

He chuckled. "You in your feelings about bullshit."

Without another word, I hit him in the mouth with my fist. He staggered backwards, but stayed on his feet. He charged toward me and we both swung at the same time. My fist hit the corner of his eye while his hit the side of my mouth. We traded fist for fist, neither of us willing to stop. I gave him a good jab to his rib cage. He followed giving me one to the nose. We were knocking over tables and chairs. Both of us were bruised and scarred from the pounding we were giving each other. I'm not surprised about Tone's ability to fight. He had a name for himself in the streets at one time. One thing I knew about fighting, never underestimate your opponent. We charged into each other and fell over some tables. We rolled around on the floor throwing fist for fist. We were finally pulled apart.

"Yo, they are going to call the cops on y'all!" King barked as he held my arms behind my back. A security guard was holding Tone.

"Man, that pic wasn't shit. You know Tawny doesn't get down like that," Tone tried to explain. I wrestled to get out of King's grip. Just to hear that nigga say her name made me want to kill him.

Everyone's eyes went to Tawny when she rushed into the club. "What are you doing?" She asked rushing over to me. She tried to touch me to observe the bruises on my face. King eased his grip and I pulled away from him.

"I'm bout to go get my dick sucked," I said walking away from her. I was so wasted I could barely walk on my own. I just know I had to get out of the sight of him and her. She followed me outside.

"Riley, you can't drive in that condition. Give me your keys!" She demanded trying to snatch my keys out my hand.

I snatched my hand back, nearly falling from my drunkenness. I laughed. "All that bullshit about wanting to build your own. You still weren't over that nigga. I'm gone let you have that. I'm a man that needs a woman that needs her man not his dick anyway. Yea, that's all you need is somebody to fuck you occasionally. Shit, everything else you can do on your own." I laughed. "You'll live a miserable, lonely life like your foster mom thinking you need to do it all on your own. I'm done with this shit!"

I tried to walk around her, but she grabbed my arm. Without thinking, I jerked away from her causing her to fall to the ground. "King, please don't let him drive!"

"Yo man, give me the keys. You know I'm not letting you drive in that condition," King said snatching the keys from my hand.

"Sit in the car until I make sure Tawny's okay," he said.

I didn't argue with him. I staggered to the passenger's side and sat down. He came back a few minutes later. "Hold still," King said turning my face to him. He took my nose between his hands and snapped it back in place. I didn't even know it was broke until he did that. I groaned out loud from the pain it caused.

"Y'all fucked each other up," he said laughing. "I guess he lived up to that reputation he once had."

I chuckled. "Nigga got some hands. I'm going to kill his ass though."

"Man, you know we don't kill over pussy." I looked at him like he was damn crazy. He knows damn well, he would kill somebody for looking at Jay too long.

He burst into laughter. "Ok my bad, but you owe him one. Remember, he saved Max's life the other night."

I had forgotten about that. "You right. My beef ain't with him anymore. It's with her. She ain't the one, man."

"Chill out. You drunk as fuck and ain't thinking straight. Sleep that shit off," he said pulling into the driveway of my home.

"I'll bring your whip back tomorrow," he said as I was getting out the car. He sat there until I entered the house. I flopped on the sofa in the den and fell asleep.

Max

"So, we gotta help them take the mothafuckas out to get the connect?" I asked as we sat in the warehouse.

"That's the deal. They are the best one to deal with. We can go another route, but prices will be higher, and they are known to be grimy."

"What's the plan? I'm in." I asked.

"You can't go. They have a mark on you if you enter Mexico or Colombia," Riley said.

"Y'all crazy as fuck if y'all think I'm staying here. This is just as much my war as it is yours," I said looking at him and Orpheus.

"Not gone happen," Orpheus said shaking his head.

"How many they ask us to bring?" Riley asked Orpheus.

"Twenty men. I'll supply ten of mine," he answered. Riley nodded his head in agreement. While they sat there discussing tactics, I was planning my own shit in my head.

We stayed at the warehouse a couple more hours getting everything in order. We ended up going to the strip club. "You plan on forgiving Tawny?" I asked Riley as we watched the boring ass stripper on the stage. She was definitely getting all ones from me.

"Nah, that's done," he said.

"Man, you know she didn't fuck that man," I said.

"It's not about that. Tawny wants her own. She doesn't want a man to provide and lead her. You know I'm not with that shit," he said. I couldn't argue with him on that.

"I'm bout to get out of here," I said standing up.

"Headed to Lexi's?" He asked.

"Nah, headed to get this shit over with my moms," I said. I had finally agreed to meet her for dinner. I gave them dap and left the club. I left the club to go see my mom. On the way I received a call from Drea to meet me at Riley's bar. I made a U-turn and headed that way. The place was empty, being it was a Wednesday night. I spotted Drea sitting at a table. I made my way over.

"What's up Gizmo?" I asked sitting down.

"Fuck you Max. You always playing," she said with an attitude.

I laughed. "What you got for me?"

"Here," she said handing me a disk.

"Who the fuck still uses disks? Why didn't you just send it to my phone?" I asked looking at the disk.

"Because that shit traceable," she said with an attitude.

"What's on it?" I asked as my phone started to ring. I knew it was my Mama.

"Hey," I said answering the call.

"I'm waiting for you," she had the nerve to say with an attitude.

"I'm going to have to take a raincheck. Something came up," I told her.

"Maxwell, I leave tomorrow," she said.

"And I'm leaving to go out of town Friday morning. I'll catch you on the next trip," I said.

"I really need to speak with you," she said in a desperate voice.

"I'll come by Granny's tomorrow. She told me you finally decided to stay with her while you were here. I guess the nice house changed your mind," I said with sarcasm. She was staying at a hotel when she first arrived. I guess seeing the big home I put Granny in changed her mind about the hotel.

"Ok, I'll see you tomorrow," she said excited. I shook my head and ended the call.

"You so damn rude," Drea said looking at me.

"What?" I asked laughing at her.

"You don't answer your phone in the middle of a conversation," she informed me.

"Man, chill out. Anyway, what's on here?"

"You wanted something to bury him. That's it. He's running for city council too. He'll never win after this leak," she said smiling.

"You work tomorrow?" I asked.

"Nah."

"I'll stop by your place tomorrow afternoon, if this is worth anything," I said holding up the disk.

"Nigga, you don't even know where I stay," she said with an attitude.

"I know everything, Gizmo," I said with a wink before getting up to leave.

My plans were to go home and watch the video, but I had to set my plan in motion for this trip to Mexico. There was no way in hell they were leaving me behind. I made all the necessary calls I needed to make. For me to make it to Mexico in a timely manner, I had to leave tomorrow evening. I didn't know if I would make it back home, so I needed one more night with her.

Lexi

I was awakened with soft, wet kisses on my back as I lay on my stomach. I should've panicked for fear of being raped, but the lips felt too familiar. The lips that I have craved since the last time they were on my body. If this was a dream, I never wanted to wake up. I slowly lifted my head to look over my shoulder. He made eye contact with me.

"Sssshhh," he said staring at me. He reached up and turned on the lamp on the night stand. "I want to memorize everything about you tonight." His hands roamed my body as he continued to bless my skin with the softest, most sensual kisses he's ever given me. His kisses trailed down to my ass cheeks. Never giving one more attention than the other, he bit them softly mixed with his wet, warm tongue. I could feel my juices spilling under me, as my pussy throbbed to feel him inside me.

"Max," I pleaded softly. As good as his tongue felt, I wanted him inside me.

"Sssshhh, I need this Lexi," he said as he massaged my ass while giving the back of my thighs the same pleasure. His tongue trailed down my legs causing goosebumps all over my body. "Turn over for me." I was more than happy to do as he said.

I turned over and stared up into his eyes. There was something different about the way he looked at me. His eyes were soft, sincere and honest. "Forget all the dumb shit I've ever did to you in the past.

Remember me from this night forward." I reached up and ran my hand from his masculine chest to his rippled stomach. He took my hand, sucking each one of my fingers into his mouth. He leaned forward sliding his tongue in my mouth. I was ravenous to taste him. I sucked his tongue into my mouth and moaned, as I enjoyed the sweetness of his saliva mixed with Cognac. I was drunk with ecstasy when he finally broke our kiss. He became more aggressive as he licked and sucked on my neck. Low groans and grunts escaped his mouth, as he licked his way down to my breast.

"Aaaahhh," I moaned with passion from the soft bites he placed on my hard nipples. He made circles around my nipples with his tongue while giving my breast a firm, sensual massage. I felt myself getting ready to explode as my hips started twirling on their own. He kissed his way down my belly until his head was between my thighs. The moment his tongue touched my drenched lips, I couldn't stand it any longer. My body stiffened and trembled. "I'm cooooomiiinnnngg!" I wailed as tears fell down the side of my face. The gentle man that started was long gone. He was now a beastly human feasting on his prey. He spread my thighs as far as they could go. I was dizzy from the orgasm that tore through me, but I could feel his tongue exploring my pussy like a cyclone. He licked, slurped and sucked me like a starved, wild animal. I came so hard I saw my cream shoot in the air when I came. My screams got stuck in my throat. My mouth was wide open with my eyes rolled back in my head. He grunted and growled as he satisfied himself with the taste of my essence. He flipped my weak body over positioning me on all fours. He spread my ass cheeks and started lapping his tongue up and down. I gasped

for my breath, from the heart stopping sensations he was giving my

body. He flipped my body back over. All I could do was lay there at

his mercy. My body and soul were his to do as he pleased. He slowly

slid his long, thick dick inside me and moaned from the pit of his

stomach.

"Fuck! You feel good!" He groaned as he slid in and out of my

soaked tunnel. He lifts my legs up as he continued to thrust inside

me, placing my feet on his chest. He started giving me slow, long

deep strokes as he licked and sucked my toes. I spoke to with him

with my eyes, because no words could come from my mouth. I was

speechless. "Come for me," he murmured staring at me as he

continued his assault on my womanhood and the pleasure to my feet.

He buried himself deep inside me hitting my soft spot. It seemed

everything went black except for the streaks of beautiful, colorful

lights dancing in the darkness as I exploded again.

"Aaarrrrggghhhh!" He howled loud enough to wake the

neighborhood as he came inside me. His head fell back as his body

shuddered and convulsed. Once he was done spilling his soul inside

of me he collapsed on top of me. We both were too drained to do

anything, but lay there. I didn't want him to move. I could feel his

heart pounding as he lay on top of me. I wanted to feel this

connection with him for as long as I could.

I awakened the next morning cradled in his strong arms. I could

live this way with him forever. I slipped out of bed and threw on my

robe. I made him a big breakfast for when he wakes up. After I was done, I went to take a shower. I smiled when I saw him open the shower door and get in with me. I took my sponge and bathed him. I started placing kisses down his chest. I gently pushed him back to sit on the shower bench. I kneeled between his legs stroking his rock-hard dick in my hand. My mouth covered the head while my tongue lapped circles around it. "Mmmmmm," he moaned gripping a handful of my plaits. I started stroking up and down his thick shaft with my tongue. I slid him into my mouth sucking him in and out of my mouth. Saliva spilled from my mouth as I continued to slurp and suck. "Fuck!" He barked as I fondled his nuts while continuing to enjoy the pleasure I was giving him. The faster I got the more he moaned, until he was pouring sweet cum down my throat.

We bathed each other again and dressed. It was weird that we hadn't had an actual conversation since he came here last night, but I felt more connected to him than I ever had. We went into the kitchen and I fixed his plate. I nibbled while he gorged on his plate. "You got any blunts rolled?" He asked with a mouth full of food.

I laughed. "No, but I can roll one for you."

I got up and retrieved my stash. I sat and rolled while he ate. Once I was done, I lit it up and took a couple of puffs before passing it to him. "Your mother keeps calling me to have dinner or something with her."

"Just tell her no," he said before taking a hit from the blunt.

"Maybe it's not a bad idea," I suggested. He gave me a look that let me know he didn't want to discuss it. I didn't want to mess up this moment, so I left it alone.

"I gotta go out of town for a few days. We'll talk when I get back," he said.

"When you leaving?"

"Tonight."

After he was done eating, he was getting ready to leave. "Come walk me to the door." I followed him to the door. He pressed his forehead against mine and gave me a kiss with just a little tongue. "You want me to face my mama. I want you to stand up to your father." I nodded my head, agreeing I would. He left me feeling like the happiest girl in the world.

<u>Tawny</u>

It's been two days since I've seen Riley and I'm about to lose my mind. I was angry with myself and him. I should've been smarter than to put myself in that situation with Tone. Riley should've trusted me to know I would never be unfaithful to him. He was more than I ever needed in a man. My thoughts went to the things he said to me that night. I started to wonder was I pushing him away, with my strong will to do everything on my own. I never discussed important decisions I made with him, because I wanted to make my own choices without anyone's help. I didn't want to feel like I had to rely on a man to achieve my goals. It's not that I don't appreciate knowing he wants to be there for me, I just had the mindset to do it myself. He was furious I signed the lease for my townhouse without discussing it with him.

"Ms. Daisy, did you ever have another boyfriend after your husband?" I asked her as we sat in her living room. She was watching some old movie and the movie was watching me. I couldn't think of anything but Riley.

"Hell no! For what?" She asked looking at as if I was crazy.

"The company, having someone to grow with, the protection and touch of a strong man," I told her.

"Chile, you better learn to do all that by yourself. These men ain't worth shit. They will use your body for all it's worth, until the next one comes along. Most of them will have you thinking you are everything to them, while fucking every loose woman that will let them. I'm glad I don't need a man for shit. I provide, protect and at one time satisfied my damn self."

"You don't miss the love?" I asked.

She laughed. "Men don't know how to love, girl. Only thing they love is their damn selves. As soon as you disagree with them or go against them, they give you their ass to kiss. That's what is wrong with women now, we don't think we can do anything without a man's love and leadership. Fuck that! After that sorry mothafucka left, I focused on me. I accomplished more in a short time, than all the years I invested in his bitch ass."

"Why did he leave?" I asked.

"Because he's a fucking man. That's what they do. They are just like stray dogs. You leave your gate open, they come in. Soon as they see a bitch in heat, they are walking back out the damn gate. I made that black bastard who he was, and he left once he got on his feet," she said with anger.

"Riley isn't like that. He loves me," I told her.

She shook her head. "Girl, that damn boy doesn't love you. He doesn't even know who he is. He only fucking you to say he a black man. He just loves black pussy."

"Riley is black," I informed her.

"Chile, I know his family. He has more colors in him than a sixty-four-color crayon box. He doesn't know what damn color he is. Poor child," she said shaking her head.

She looked at me. "He done left yo ass ain't he?"

"No, we just having some issues," I lied.

"What kind of issues?"

"He thinks I'm messing with Tone," I said in a low voice. I knew she was about to go off.

"You're bout one dumb ass heifer to be so pretty. I guess you can't have it all these days. It's a sin to eat your own vomit," she said.

"What?" I asked confused.

"You had that boy in your gut. You realized he wasn't shit and threw him up, now you are going back to lick him up," she said shaking her head. "Besides, ain't that boy on crack rock?"

"Not anymore. He's doing good for himself. I'm not messing with him though. We're just friends," I explained.

"Once a crack head, always a crack head," she said.

"Chile, let me tell you something. You better stop focusing on these no-good men. Build a life for yourself. Don't put your heart into a man. They will take you down, where you feel like you need them. Never put yourself in a position to need a damn man. That's what they want you to do, so they can do whatever the fuck they want. They want you in the position to feel like you must put up with their shit. I raised you to be a self-reliant, strong, black woman and got damn it, you better never let a man feel like you can't do it without him," she said staring at me with a stern face. I nodded my head in agreement.

After spending a little more time with Ms. Daisy, I decided to see if Riley would talk to me now. I was hoping he had calmed down enough to hear what I had to say. He wasn't home, so I hit up a few spots where I know he usually is. I had no luck finding him, and all my calls went unanswered. I can't believe this was happening to me. Just when it seemed I was getting everything I ever wanted, I lose the one person that would make it all possible. The more I thought about it, the angrier I became. I don't understand how he could walk away from me so easily. Maybe Ms. Daisy was right. Maybe his love for me wasn't what I thought it was.

Tone

"How long are you going to be gone?" Toya asked as I got dressed.

"I don't know. Should be only a few days," I told her.

"I'm not stupid Tone. I know there's something you are not telling me," she said with an attitude. I had to chuckle at her. Toya's entire attitude has changed lately, and I like it. She speaks her mind more and doesn't let my slick shit fly, without going ham on my ass.

"Jiera is going to come over and help you put all this paperwork on the laptop I bought you. That should keep you busy until I get back."

"What about the job you have here?" She asked.

"The foreman is handling things until I get back," I assured her.

She flopped down on the bed. "I am enrolling in school. I'm going for business management."

I winked and smiled at her. "That's good baby girl. You can help me manage the business." She giggled and blushed.

I walked to her and kneeled between her legs. "When I get back, we are going to sit down and discuss some shit. It's time for some changes." She nodded her head in agreement. I don't give a damn what she says, she's moving her ass to Minnesota with my daughter. Toya was sweet and naïve when I met her. She was quiet and shy. She had just broken up with her boyfriend, who she found out was fucking her mother. The more I was around her the more I was drawn to her. I was going through shit with Tawny and taking more drugs than I could handle when I met her. She made me feel like a man, even at my lowest point. She never looked down or disrespected me. She was the quiet girl in her family. She came from a loud, ghetto ass family. Her sister helped, if there was money in it for her. I picked Lucindy up out of her playpen placing kisses all over her face as she giggled. I placed her in Toya's lap and gave her a long passionate kiss before leaving. I needed to check on the job site and stop by to see Jay. After checking on the job, I went to Jiera's store.

She shook her head at me as she sorted a rack of clothes as I walked in the store. "I didn't do anything." I said throwing my hands.

"I told you to stay away from her," she said walking to the back of the store. I followed behind her to her office.

"We just had a couple of drinks and talked about old times," I explained sitting on the couch.

"Whatever Tone, I know you had other intentions in mind with her," she said rolling her eyes at me, as she sat behind her desk.

I chuckled. "You right I did, but I realized that shit I felt was the memories I had with her. I still felt fucked up about the way I did her. I guess I needed to say my piece to her."

"And the fighting?" She asked.

I shrugged. "We fought. As far as I'm concerned, it's over. Nigga fucked up my ribs, though."

"What?" She asked with concern.

"I'm good, just bruised up pretty damn bad," I said touching my side. I didn't realize how bad I was fucked up until I got home. Toya made me go to the ER to make sure they weren't broken.

"I know Toya's mad at you," she said shaking her head.

I smiled. "She was. We are making up," I said with a wink.

"Tone, if you don't mean that girl any good let her go," she advised me with a serious face.

"I don't know Jay, I'm feeling something different with her. She's changing, and I like it," I told her.

"Hanging with sis n law," she said with a smile.

"I should've damn known you was in her ear. She's starting to act just like your ass," I said shaking my head. She burst into laughter.

"Listen, I'm going out of town for a few days. Jay, don't freak out when I say this shit," I warned her.

"What?" she asked with concerned eyes.

"Just promise me, you'll look out for them if something happens to me. I have a couple accounts set up for them. Here's the info," I said sliding the envelope over to her.

"What's going on Tone?"

"It's nothing like that. I'm good. I'm just helping someone out," I said. She still looked worried. "I promise Jay. I'm not fucking up." Her body relaxed.

"Tone this is a big insurance policy. How did you get this?" She asked.

"Unc hooked me up," I said smiling.

"Look at you being all grown and responsible," she said smiling. It felt good to see my sister proud of me. After giving Jay a big hug I headed to my destination.

I made a pit stop to get something to eat. It was a small, family owned bar-be-cue place that I used to love to come eat at. The moment I stepped out my car, I knew it was going to be bullshit. I came face to face with one of the hustlers I fucked over when I was using. He was smiling as he approached me. "What up Nigga?" He asked standing face to face with me. "You got my money?" I had his money, but I didn't like the way he was standing in front of me. He stood there like I was to respect and fear his punk ass.

"Charge that shit to the game," I said attempting to walk around him. He tried to swing on me. I blocked his jab and punched him in the face. He stumbled back trying to pull his gun out. Before he could get it out, mine was sitting on his third eye. "Mothafucka, I ain't that nigga." He raised his hands up to surrender. I reached in my pocket with my other hand and threw a wad of cash at him. "That should cover it." I hit him with the butt of the gun knocking him out. I walked in the restaurant and ordered my food. When I came out, some dude was helping him get up. I knew I made some enemies, before leaving. I was prepared to handle all of them accordingly.

Max

I hated to leave Lexi. I'm going to make this shit right with her when I return, if she's willing to give me another chance. I know Riley and Orpheus going to be mad as hell when I show up. There's no way I was letting my family go into a war zone without me. I walked into my Granny's house surprised to find it empty. I figured she was in her bedroom. I headed up the stairs and could hear voices. The closer I got, I realized it was Granny and my Mama.

"I don't have that kind of money," Granny expressed to her.

"Ask him, he will give it to you. He hates me. He will never help me," Mama said with a broken voice.

"And exactly what am I going to tell him I need $200,000 for?"

"I don't know. Make up something. They're going to kill us if he doesn't come up with the money," Mama said in frustration.

I walked into the bedroom. "All that bullshit about wanting to have a relationship with me was about wanting to get money from me?"

"No, I promise Maxwell. It isn't. I want us to have a relationship, but I'm in trouble and I don't have anyone to turn to," she said with a wet face as she walked toward me.

I took a few steps back. "You think I would help you when you left me to die?"

"I'm sorry. I just couldn't take it anymore."

"And you thought a little boy could?" I barked at her causing her to jump.

"He wouldn't let me come back to get you. I wanted to, but he didn't want the trouble with your father," she tried to explain.

"Being a mother, that's when you should've told that nigga to kiss yo ass," I told her.

"Please Maxwell, we have to have the money before midnight tomorrow. He has a gambling problem and owes some very bad people," she explained.

"You must be out of your damn mind if you think I will give you a damn dime," I said staring her in the eyes. She burst into tears dropping to the floor on her knees. I felt no remorse for her. I walked out the bedroom wanting to get the hell away from her selfish ass.

"Maxwell, stop!" Granny yelled as I walked out the front door of her house. I stopped like she demanded.

"Baby look at me," she ordered in her soft, motherly voice. I turn to face her. "That hate you have for her will eat you alive. Let that negative energy go, baby. I'm not asking you to love or forgive her for her. I'm asking you to do it for yourself."

"You want me to give her the money?" I asked in disbelief.

She started to cry. "She's my child. I don't know how to do anything but love, flaws and all." I closed my eyes, hating to see my Granny like this. She was pleading for her daughter's life. It made me think of Maxi. I knew there wasn't a damn thing she could do on this earth to make me not love her.

"I'm not helping her, you can," I told her.

"Baby, I don't have that kind of money," she explained.

"Yes, you do Granny. The account I opened for you a few months ago. It has the money in it. Don't give her no more than she needs. Don't tell her about the account," I advised her.

"I remember that account. You brought the information to me. It only had a couple of thousand in it," she said with a puzzled look on her face.

"It's an overseas account. The interest rate was damn good," I said winking at her.

She wrapped her motherly arms around me and wept. "Thank you, baby." I hugged her with the same love she had given me over the years.

"This for you, not her," I reminded her. "I'm going out of town for a few days. I told Lexi to come check on you."

"Y'all back together?" She asked enthused.

"Work in progress," I told her.

I was pushing for time and needed to see Drea. I called her and told her to meet me at Riley's bar. I headed that way. I took a seat in the back of the bar drinking a beer, waiting on Drea. After fifteen minutes, I started to get impatient. Just as I was getting up to leave, she came walking in the bar. "Damn Gizmo, what took you so long?"

"Shut up fool. I was busy," she said sitting at the table.

"Oh, thought maybe somebody fed your ass after midnight and turned you into one of those evil ass Gremlins," I said with a smile. I loved fucking with Drea. She wasn't one of those sensitive females that didn't know how to take a joke.

"Ugh, I don't know how Lexi deals with you," she said wanting to laugh at my joke.

"Because she loves me," I said smiling. "Here, that was some good info. It'll hit the internet in a few days." I slid her a thick envelop.

"Damn, I wasn't expecting this. A bitch about to go shopping," she said excitedly as she danced in her chair. I laughed, but it was immediately cut short when I saw Lexi and Tawny headed our way. Lexi eyes met mine and I knew this was about to all go downhill.

"I fucking hate you!" She screamed as she attacked me. She was swinging and clawing on me like a big ass panther. Tawny stood back with her arms crossed. "You ain't shit nigga!"

"Come on Lexi, that's enough," Tawny said pulling her off me.

"Lexi, this ain't what it looks like. I would never do that to you," Drea tried to explain.

"Bitch, shut up before I whoop yo ass!" Lexi said staring at Drea with fire in her eyes.

"Lexi for real, this shit business. I'm not bullshitting you this time," I pleaded with her standing up from the table.

"I fell for all that love shit last night. You don't love me. You don't even know how to love yourself," she said with hate, hurt and love in her eyes. She hit a nerve with that statement.

I laughed. "Meet my father hell! I would never bring a piece of shit like you to meet a man like my father. You don't deserve to breathe the same air as him."

"That's enough Lexi," Tawny said pulling her by the arm.

"Yea, get her the fuck outta here before shit gets worse," I said never taking my eyes of Lexi. She cut me deep with those words. All the shit I've done to her she's never said any fucked-up shit like that to me. I watched her walk out the bar with my soul still inside her.

"Let her calm down. I'll explain this shit to her later," Drea said.

"Do whatever you want," I said walking away. I understood now how words can cut deeper than anything sometimes.

Riley

"What up Pops?" I asked stepping up on my parent's porch. Pops was sitting out on the porch in his rocking chair being nosey.

"Expenses," he said as he rocked. My dad was a dentist. He had a successful practice.

"You need something. You know I got you," I told him.

"Boy, I'm good. You asked what was up and I answered. It doesn't mean I'm broke," he said with a smile.

"Oh ok, well just know the offer is always there," I reminded him.

"You about done with that side business. I see you a legit business man too. You got bars, restaurants, car washes and dealerships," he said.

"I'm working on it. I'm not going to do it forever. I know how you feel about it."

"Once you turned eighteen, you had the right to make your own decisions. I know we had our issues before that, but you turned out good son. I'm proud of you," he said giving me a head nod. I've never been the type of nigga to cry, but hearing my old man say those words meant the world to me. He was disappointed in me when he found out I was hustling. We had arguments about it until I turned eighteen and moved out. His only request was that I finish school and I did. I even took some college classes to get a degree in Business Management.

"Thanks Pop?" I said with a smile.

"What you sitting out here watching?" I asked. He was a nosey man.

"Them fast ass sisters across the street. The moment Martha and Charles pulled out the drive way, two lil nappy headed boys went in the house. I got a good mind to call Charles and tell him," he said looking over at the house.

I laughed. "Leave them young folks alone. Where's Mom?"

"Went to play Bingo with Virginia. How's that fine ass girlfriend of yours?" He asked with a smile.

I shook my head. "It didn't work out."

He gave me a disappointed look. "Damn, I hate to hear that. I liked her. She was pretty, smart and ambitious."

"Too ambitious," I said shaking my head.

"What's wrong with that?" He asked.

"She's that independent woman that doesn't want a man to lead her," I explained.

"Nah, she doesn't seem like that type. I observed her. She seems to respect you as the man in the relationship," he said.

"She isn't ready for what I want. She wants to achieve all her goals without my support, before we start building something together."

He chuckled. "You are your father's son. Your mother wanted to go to college. I told her to let me finish first then she could go. By the time I finished, she was happy being a homemaker. There's nothing wrong with her wanting to achieve her goals. You help lead her to them. Don't feel like she's taking your manhood because she wants to have her own. As long as she makes you feel needed and loved, everything is good."

"That's the problem. I feel loved, but not needed," I explained.

He nodded his head. "Have you discussed that with her?"

I laughed. "Kinda. I got wasted the other night and said it in a messed-up way." He shook his head and laughed.

"Communication and Compromise," he said winking at me. I nodded my head letting him know I understand.

I sat and talked with him for another hour. I went by King's house to let him know everything was set up for tomorrow. He wasn't a part of this trip, but I wanted him to be in the loop. Even though he turned his empire over to us, I still felt he deserved to know what was going on. He wasn't happy about being excluded from the trip, but it was for the best. I have been calling Max all day, but he's not answering. I know he's mad about not going with us. He was a marked man and could easily be recognized. We weren't willing to take that chance.

After leaving King's house, I headed to my bar to finish up some paperwork before heading home to get some rest. Honestly, I was trying to keep myself busy, to keep from thinking about Tawny. I don't know what she was thinking meeting Tone. Regardless if something happened or not, there was a reason she felt like she had to meet him. If she had unresolved feelings for him, I know I'm not the nigga for her. As much as I love her, I wasn't going to fight for her to stay with me knowing, I've done everything to love her the way she deserves.

I grabbed a bottle from behind the counter and headed to my office. After about an hour of drinking straight Cognac, the screen on the computer started to get blurry. I knew it was time to take my ass home and get some sleep. My dick started to get hard, thinking about burying myself deep inside Tawny for the rest of the night. I left out the back entrance where my car was parked. Just as I was cranking up Sherry jumped in the passenger seat.

"Man, what the fuck you doing?" I asked.

"Going home with you," she said trying to look sexy. Sherry was sexy as hell with her milk chocolate, smooth skin and fat ass. We were a thing at one time, but it didn't work out. I just wasn't feeling her on that level. She had her own business selling hair and did pretty good. She was just too childish for me. She was always on social media arguing and causing drama. She still does to this day. After I ended things with her, she started acting a complete fool. She was arguing and fighting with every girl she thought I was fucking.

She leaned over putting her head in my lap. I know I shouldn't be doing this, but my dick was already hard as fuck. Just when she was pulling my dick out the passenger door flew open and Sherry was being yanked out the car. I looked in disbelief as Tawny started whooping her ass. I'm talking she was beating her like a man. All she could do was cover her face to avoid the blows she was getting. I hopped out the car. It took me a couple minutes to pull her off Sherry. Sherry's face was fucked up.

"That bitch knocked my teeth out," she said crying as blood poured out her mouth. I wanted to tell her you should see the rest of your face.

Tawny jerked away from me. "Now, you can have the bitch!" All I could do was stand there and wonder what the fuck just happened.

"I'm suing that bitch," Sherry said crying.

"You ain't doing shit. Here that should cover the damages to your face," I said throwing her all the cash out my wallet. I left her standing there in the parking lot. I burst into laughter as I drove home thinking about how Tawny whooped her ass. I wanted to go over to her house, but I knew better. I'd handle her when I get back in town.

Lexi

"**L**exi, open the damn door. I know you are home!" Drea yelled as she banged on my door. I snatched the door opened and stared at her.

"You come to my house to take your ass whooping?" I asked.

"Girl move, you ain't beating nobody ass," she said pushing me out the way and walking in my condo.

"I swear Drea, get the fuck out. I'm too emotionally drained to fight you right now," I told her. "I don't have the mindset to deal with anymore lies. If you fucking him, just do it. Just please, don't come in my face and deny that shit."

"Girl let me hold you. You need a hug," she said walking up to me with her arms open. Honestly, I did. I refuse to cry last night, and I still haven't. I don't even know if I can cry over him anymore. I pushed her back.

"Girl, I can't stand that aggravating ass boy that you love so much. I wouldn't fuck him with yo pussy," she said laughing.

I stared at her to see if she was lying. "What were you doing there with him?"

"Business. Payback for you," she said smiling. I gave her a puzzled look. "I told you I had something for Randall."

"What does Max have to do with that?" I asked. She explained to me what happened.

"He did that for me?" I asked feeling awful for the things I said to him.

"Paid me ten grand," she said as she twerked. I don't know where it came from, but I burst into tears.

"I was so mean to him," I said as I cried.

She held me. "Girl, that ignorant fool loves you. He'll be aight." She didn't understand how deep my words were to him. I knew what I was doing when I said those things. I wanted him to feel how I was feeling at that moment.

"I have to go find him and apologize," I said breaking our embrace.

"You can't, he's gone out of town," she informed me.

"Damn, I forgot."

"Just suck his dick like a porn star when he comes back," she said smiling. She made me laugh.

"I'm sorry Drea," I said sincerely.

"It's all good. I would've done the same thing," she said smiling.

Drea stayed and kept me companying for a while. After she left, I decided to go check on Ms. Violet. I got dressed and made my way over to her house. I knocked on the door and was surprised to see Max's mother answer the door. I thought she was leaving today. "Hi, is Ms. Violet here?"

"No, she went to the store come on in," she said moving to the side to let me in.

"If you're looking for Max, he's out of town," she said as I followed her into the living room.

"No, I just came by to see Ms. Violet," I said taking a seat.

"How are you?" She asked.

"I'm fine. I thought you were leaving today."

"I decided to stay a while longer. Hopefully, to build a relationship with my son. Maybe you can help me with that," she said smiling. "Oh, where are my manners? Would you care for something to drink?"

"No thank you."

"I was thinking maybe you could talk to Max about the importance of having a good relationship with your parents," she said.

The words came out of my mouth before I knew it. "Maybe that should've been something to consider before you left him."

She looked at me in shock. "I had no choice. His father was an abusive man."

"And you left your only child there with him. How could you?" I asked. I was disgusted with her lack of remorse for what she had done.

"I thought he would stop once I was gone."

"You gambled with his life to save yours," I told her.

"You don't know the situation I was in. You don't have the right to judge me for my choices. No one understands what he was doing to me."

I stared at her. "Not once have you mentioned what he was doing to him while you were there. You knew what he was capable of." I stood up to leave. I couldn't stand to be around her any longer. "You are right though. There was no choice. Your choice should have been your child."

"You will never be happy with him as long as he has that hate in his heart. This will help you too," she said.

"I will not use his love for me to help you. If he chooses to welcome you back into his life, it will be his own choice. Honestly, I don't see how it would benefit him having you back in his life," I said walking out the house and to my car. *The nerve of her.*

<u>Max</u>

Mexico

"My cousin whooped yo ass, didn't he?" I asked Tone as we sat in the hotel room. "Yo cousin got his ass whooped," he said holding his side.

I laughed. "Why you holding your side then?"

"What kind of cat attacked yo ass?" He asked laughing, looking at the aftermath of Lexi's anger on my face.

"She couldn't handle my pussy eating skills and lost control," I said smiling.

"Nigga shut the fuck up. You been talking since we got on the plane. Did you ask him how his nose got broken?" He asked in frustration.

I burst into laughter. "Aight, I'll give it to you. You got heart."

"What's the damn plan from here?" He asked.

"I got somebody letting me know when they making their move. We sit tight until it happens."

"How you get the private jet?" He asked.

"I know some people that know some people," I said smiling.

"You annoying as fuck," he said shaking his head.

"One of my customers let me use his," I informed him.

I wasn't going to let them know I was here until the last minute. If I told them now, they would hold me hostage in this room. Tone agreed to come with me to give us more man power. Tone went to take a shower and I relaxed on the bed. We weren't in a five-star hotel. I wanted to be low key and not raise suspicion. Two black men checking into an expensive ass hotel raises red flags. My mind wondered to Lexi as I relaxed. She was calling and texting me, but I didn't answer. She apologized for the shit she said. One thing about words, once they leave your mouth there's no taking them back.

"Hey," I answered my burner phone when it rang.

"It's going down tomorrow night. I'll hit you back up with the meeting spot tomorrow. They are going there in a couple of hours, pretending to be interested in copping from them. They'll be scoping shit out," he informed me.

"I need to know the fucking lay out too," I told him.

"Ok, calm down. I will be there once it turns dark. I will take you. We can't get to close though, they have high security," he informed me.

"We'll be waiting," I said ending the call.

After Tone got out the shower, I told him the plan. I went to my room and chilled until my resource showed up to take us to scope out the area. I started thinking about how my mama came back to town trying to give a damn about me. Her only goal was to get money out of me. I remember the day she left. It was the morning after my Daddy had beat her ass and then mine for no reason. He was smart enough to never put bruises on my face, but she had a black eye and busted lip. She promised me she would come back. She never did. He came home drunk as usual later that night. When he realized she was gone, he took his anger out on me. I couldn't sleep on my back for nearly a week. I don't understand how a parent could leave their child in a situation like that. I closed my eyes tight to fight back the images of his beatings in my head.

Riley

"Everybody ready?" I asked as we stood around in the warehouse about fifty men deep. We had enough ammunition to take out ISIS. We had a meeting with Juan and Felipé yesterday. They were discussing becoming our connect and we were scoping out the layout. They had the home locked down, but we were coming through fully loaded.

José was going to be our new connect. King knew him from dealings with his father. His father retired and turned the business over to him. He was giving us the same price as the Santiago family. He recently learned the Valdez boys were planning to take over his organization also. No one had proof they killed the Santiago's, but everyone knew it was them. They were malicious and cold blooded. There was no trust or loyalty in their family. I refused to work with anyone like that.

"Yea, we all good," his man in charge said cocking his gun. We all immediately turned to the door with our guns pointed when it started to open. Everyone was already here, so no one should've been coming through the door.

"What's up cousin?" Max said walking in with a big ass gun and smile on his face.

"Man, you so damn hard headed," I said shocked, but happy to see him.

"You know damn well I wasn't missing this party," he said giving Orpheus dap first.

"What the fuck happened to your face?" Orpheus asked staring at him. He had long scratches all over his face and a cut on his lip.

He chuckled. "My pussy eating skills a beast."

I laughed. "Nigga stop lying. Lexi done caught your ass doing some dumb shit again."

He laughed. "Not exactly. Anyway, what's the plan?" I looked at Orpheus for his opinion of letting him come along. He shrugged his shoulders. I nodded for him to follow me to the table. We had a model setup of how we planned to enter. Orpheus and I will already be in the house as guest. The rest of the team will be positioned outside.

"Hold on," Max said before pulling out his burner phone. "Yea, come on in." I looked at him as if he was crazy wondering who the fuck was he inviting in here. I was nearly knocked off my feet when Tone came walking through the door.

"Man, what the fuck this nigga doing here?" I asked with anger.

"Man power. He gotta killer's aim," Max said.

"Ain't no damn way I'm going into battle with this nigga with a gun. I'll be trying to kill them while he has the gun to my back," I told them.

"That shit dead, man. We fought, it's over," Tone said staring at me. I understood what he was saying, but I didn't want the nigga on my team.

"Yea, it's over but you still ain't in this," I said staring at him.

"Shit, he's here. We can use all the manpower we can get," Orpheus chimed in.

I stared at Tone for a few seconds. "Nigga don't stand behind me. I wanna be able to see you at all times." He laughed and nodded his head.

"We bout to head out. Y'all coming through about an hour after we leave. Sanchez, will lay everything out for y'all," I told them as me and Orpheus prepared to leave. The moment we took a step, the warehouse door came open.

"Oh, hell nah!" I barked when King came walking inside.

Max laughed. "This like that movie, Dead Presidents. Seems like we put an ad in the paper for this hit." Everyone just stared at him. "Fuck y'all!" He said waving us off.

"Come on bro, you know this ain't the place for you," I told King.

"Man, I wasn't planning on coming until last night. Jiera up crying all night about some shit this nigga into. I put that shit together and brought my ass here," he explained.

"Man, you can't be in on this. This ain't your life anymore," Orpheus reminded him.

"But this my family forever. Shit, I gotta bring this pencil head nigga back home to his sister, or I'll never get peace or pussy in my house again," he said. We all laughed.

"You sure about this?" I asked staring at him.

He chuckled. "While y'all in here planning shit. I got like fifteen men sitting on the house right now."

"My nigga!" Max roared lifting his hand to give King dap. King gave him that look. "My bad, I mean my black brother." He laughed and gave him dap.

"King, you rolling with us or going with them?" I asked.

"I'll roll with them. They killed some loyal friends of mine. I take that shit personal," he said. I nodded my head in agreement.

"Aight, we out," I told them. We left everyone at the warehouse for our destination.

<u>Tone</u>

"How the hell you let this fool convince you to come with him?" King asked looking at me and Max.

Max threw his arm around my shoulder. "This my new BFF since he saved my life."

I slung his arm from around me. "I swear y'all need to get this nigga a check. He's some kind of special. He just better run me my money when we get home."

"I gotcha best friend," Max said with a smile. King laughed. Only Max would be happy and hyped about going into a gun battle. I can honestly say he's calm down since he was first released from prison. I remember hearing about him dismembering bodies with a smile on his face and a hard dick.

"Aight, let's load up and get out of here," King ordered. Everyone started walking out the warehouse. I was walking beside King when his body hit the floor. He was knocked out cold. I turned and stared at Max ready to body his ass. He was standing there with a four by four board in his hand.

"This ain't his fight. He's come too far to get tied up in this," he said shrugging his shoulders.

"Man, he's going to kill yo ass when he wakes up," I warned him.

"Shit, somebody gotta live to tell the story," he said smiling.

"You are fuckin' retarded," I said shaking my head. I bent down to make sure King was okay. He was just knocked out cold. We locked him in the warehouse and headed out.

We drove toward our destination in silence. I noticed a complete change in Max's behavior. He was in a zone. He just stared with a blank expression on his face. I left him to his thoughts. I guess this was his way of preparing himself for battle. Once we arrived, we staked out in the woods surrounding the huge mansion with the men King already had in place. Everyone knew once the clock struck ten o'clock pm, we were to start moving in. We had three minutes left.

Soon as ten o'clock came we moved out of the woods spraying gunfire everywhere. We caught them off guard, but they started firing bullets along with us. Some of their men were dropping as well as ours. We were trying to make it to the inside of the house as quick as possible. I motioned for Max to take his crew on toward the house while we handled the outside. We got closer to the house as bodies continued to fall. I saw Max and his men bust down the front door firing bullets as they entered the house. I rushed up the stairs to follow them. Bodies were laid throughout the house.

"They went into a tunnel while we were taking out the security," Orpheus said. We followed him in the direction they went. I was relieved to see him and Riley still alive. I wanted all of us to walk out of here with our lives. The tunnel was dark. We could barely see our way through. There were different directions we could take. We split up in pairs with soldiers following behind us. Once Max and turned a corner bullets started flying past our head. That nigga had

Rebellious: A Rebel Spin-Off Nona Day

some kind of death wish. He held up his two machine guns and started flying bullets everywhere as he walked toward the area the bullets were coming from. He was dropping bodies as we continued to fire at them. We finally caught up to Juan running down the tunnel. I fired hitting him in the leg. Max had told me he wanted to look him in the eye when he killed him, so I only wounded him. Max ran up to him and kicked him in the side.

"You put a mark on my life you bitch ass nigga," I said as he continued to kick him.

"Yo, we don't have time for this shit. There's still gunfire down here. We need to see what's up," I told him. He turned him and stared in the face. He kept shooting Juan in the face until he literally had no head. I don't mean his face was gone. His entire head was blown away. We rushed in the opposite direction. "Yo!" I yelled trying to get the location of Orpheus and Riley.

"This way," Orpheus called out. We made our way to them. They were cornered off and outnumbered. We started jumping bodies again. They came out killing the last few men that were closer to them.

"Where is Felipé?" Max asked looking around at the bodies.

"Dead," Riley said as we made our way out the tunnels and outside. I hated some of our soldiers died, but most of us were living with our lives. Me and Riley went back into the main house to make sure everyone was dead while Max and Orpheus surveyed the outside.

We were in the huge living area when three men walked in with their guns pointed at us. We both looked at each other knowing we were fucked. If we raised our guns we were dead. "Fuck!" He said under his breath. In no time, shots fired, and their bodies dropped to the floor. We looked up to see King standing there holding a machine gun.

"The next bullets for yo crazy fuckin' ass," King said with a scowl on his face. I had to laugh. Orpheus and Max came rushing into the house.

"Fool, you knocked me out!" King roared staring at Max with a frown on his face.

"But did you die?" Max asked with a smile. King let off one shot shooting him in the thigh.

"Fuccckkk!" Max howled in pain. "Man, I was just looking out for you!" We all stood there quietly watching Max hopping around in pain. We couldn't hold it any longer. We all burst out laughing.

We all loaded back up. King called a doctor to come remove the bullet from Max's leg. After making sure he was okay, I went to my room to crash. Riley, King and Orpheus went to meet with their new connect. I was ready to get back home to my family. They can have this life.

Tawny

"I would've paid anything to see you whooping her ass," Jiera said as we sat in her den. I found out that Sherry was the one that sent Riley the pictures of me and Tone through mutual acquaintances. I was at the club looking for Riley that night. The bartender told me he had just left out the back door. I saw Sherry sitting in the car with him when I walked out. I became furious when I saw her head go down. I tried to beat the life out of her. I wondered was he still messing with her the entire time. Everything Ms. Daisy was saying to me was coming true. My only focus from this point on is myself.

"I can't believe he was tripping about a picture when he was still fucking that bitch," I said to her and Lexi. Lexi was sitting there playing with Mufasa.

"You don't know if he's been messing with her for sure, Tawny," Lexi said. "Look how I fucked up Max's face, because I jumped to conclusions."

"He deserved that ass whooping anyway for previous fuck ups," Jiera said laughing.

"That's true," Lexi said with a laugh.

"I said some mean things to him though. Hurtful things," she said with remorse.

"Well for once, looks like you'll be doing the begging," I said smiling at her.

"JR, pass me that wine" Lexi said with a fretful look. "I need something to drink."

"You still haven't told your dad you lost your job yet?" Jiera asked.

"No, I don't want to hear his mouth. Can you imagine him if I told him I was giving strip and pole dancing lessons?" Jiera and I laughed. We knew how her father was and he probably would have a heart attack on the spot.

"What will your mother say about you starting your own business?" I asked.

"Whatever my father says," she answered rolling her eyes.

"Why aren't you drinking?" Jiera asked Tawny.

She shrugged her shoulders. "Just not in the mood." Jiera stared at me and I knew I was busted. I wanted to keep my secret, because at this point I didn't know what I wanted to do.

"Oh my God! You're pregnant!" Jiera jumped up screaming. She knew I didn't turn down wine. Especially King's expensive wine he kept in his cellar.

"What?" Lexi asked confused.

I dropped my head. It had to have happened in Jamaica. I forgot to take my pills with me. I figured since I've been on them so long, I wouldn't get pregnant. I was highly mistaken. I realized yesterday, that I hadn't seen my period. I rushed and purchased a few tests. After taking all of them, I knew I was pregnant. I always thought of having Riley's child. The place we are at now isn't the best time for me to be pregnant. Jiera and Lexi hugged me congratulated me, while I pondered whether I wanted to keep it or not.

"Riley is going to be ecstatic," Jiera said with a big grin.

"I have to go to the doctor to make sure I am. I'm late and that's something that never happens. I took a few tests and they all say positive. I don't know if I'm keeping it. I don't even know if our relationship is over or not. Plus, I have things I want to do before having a child," I told them.

"You going to have an abortion?" Lexi asked with disappointment on her face.

"I'm considering it, so don't say anything about it," I said looking at them.

"Don't say anything about what?" Angel asked walking in the den. She took Mufasa out of her Lexi's lap and sat next to me. We all sat there quietly. "What did I walk in on?"

"Tawny's pregnant and she's thinking about having an abortion," Jiera blurted out. I gave her an ugly look. "I'm sorry. She always makes me confess things so easily."

I glanced at Angela. "Why don't you want it?"

"It's not that I don't want it. I'm just not sure if this is the best time. Our relationship is rocky, and I wanted to open my second studio before having a baby," I explained.

"What's stopping you from doing it all? You have a strong man, loving friends to help you whenever you need it," Angela said.

"Tawny doesn't want Riley's help in accomplishing her goals. She wants to do it herself," Lexi said.

Angela looked at me as if I was crazy. "Girl, if you don't stop with that independent woman bullshit. If that man wants to help you, let him. Not allowing him to be the man he was raised to be is like taking his manhood. This country already devalues a black man. The last thing he needs is to give his heart to a woman that does the same. Eventually, he will start to feel as if he is useless to you. I don't have to tell you, the next thing he will do is find a woman that does."

"He already feels that way," I confessed with shame.

"Fix that shit! I'm not saying you got to depend on him to provide for you. I'm saying let that man know he is needed. If he doesn't feel needed by you, he will find someone that does need him," she said scolded me like a child. "Y'all young girls kill me. Walking y'all asses 'round here with that I don't need a man attitude. The moment a good man comes along, you run him off with that independent shit. Soon as no good nigga comes, you'll go broke trying to keep him there. Stop listening to your crazy ass God Mama. I know that's where you're getting that shit from. Her story is not yours Tawny." She was mad.

"I just don't want to feel like without him I won't have anything," I explained.

"You finished school and opened your own studio without him. Now you have him to help you accomplish more. Let him do that. You can have this baby and open your second studio, if you sit yo ass down with your man and compromise," she said.

"Girl, you done ran my pressure up. Got me cussing in front of my grandbaby," she said kissing on the baby's fat cheeks. Lexi and Jiera giggled.

"And you, let me find out you are putting yo hands on that man again. I don't give a damn what he did. Don't hit a man unless you wanna get hit back. If he keeps breaking your heart, hurt him in the worst way possible. Walk the fuck away and never look back. You got the "break up to make up" song confused. You have a disagreement, discuss it and make up. It's not cheat, fight and make up," she said staring at Lexi. It was my time to giggle. Lexi just nodded her head like a little child.

"How you know about Lexi fighting Max?" Jiera asked.

"I keep up with y'all lil heifers," she said with a wink. We all laughed. "Now, go pack my Grandbaby's bag. He's staying with me for a few days," she told Jiera. Jiera walked out the room to get Mufasa's things together.

Lexi

I've still been trying to call Max, but he's still not answering his phone. I know he's back in town, because Jiera told me. It's been two days since Angela scolded us like we were little girls. His mother hadn't reached out to me anymore. Whenever I go to see Ms. Violet, she's never there. Ms. Violet said she don't think she's planning on going back to her husband. I guess since he is broke, she has no use for him. I don't see Max ever forgiving her. When she talks about the past, it's never about him. It's all about what she went through. Today was the day I was going to tell my parents about losing my job. I took a deep breath before exiting my car. My mommy and daddy were in the den watching television. I walked in and flopped down on the sofa.

"Hey baby, how was work?" Ma asked. I shrugged my shoulders. I wasn't going to open my mouth until Asia was here with me.

"Hey Daddy," I said looking at him.

"He gave me a smile. "I have a nice, young man for you to meet. It's time you considered marriage. You've finished school and started you're career. With the help of a successful husband, I'm sure you can be the director of nursing in no time."

"Daddy, I'm not thinking of marrying anyone yet," I said.

He was about to speak when Asia walked into the den. I breathed a sigh of relief. "Hey family," she said sounding cheerful. "Guess what?"

Everyone looked at her as she stood in front of all of us. "What is it baby? Must be good news. You look so happy," Mommy said smiling up at her.

"Hopefully, this one is getting married to a successful man," Daddy said.

"Nope, I'm gay," Asia said with a smile. I burst into laughter. I knew she wasn't gay. The look on our parent's face was priceless. "I'm just kidding." My parents breathed a sigh of relief.

"I quit my job today," she said excited. My mouth dropped open. I thought she was coming as my support, not to join me in giving our parents a heart attack.

"What?" Daddy barked lifting from his recliner.

"What in the world are you thinking, Asia?" Mommy asked with wide eyes.

"I don't like being a nurse. I love doing hair. I'm going to open my own shop," she said with confidence.

She gave me the confidence I needed to speak. "I lost my job a few weeks ago. I'm going to start my own business doing makeup."

"The hell you are! Neither one of you are ruining a perfectly good career to go pursue some pipe dream," Daddy demanded.

"Daddy, we aren't happy being nurses. We were blessed with a gift and we want to use it. All our lives we have done what you wanted. We had to follow in our sister's footsteps to meet your approval. Whatever we do, never measures up to your standards. What good is it to make you happy when we aren't happy?" I explained to him.

"I'm trying to lead you all down the right path. It's obvious you don't have the mindset to do that for yourselves. You two have always been stubborn. You think you can become rich doing hair and makeup. That's not a successful career. Anyone can do that."

"It's not about becoming rich. It's about being happy doing what we love to do," Asia chimed in.

"I will not let you ruin your future's this way. Ava talk to your children," he demanded turning to face our mother.

"I'm proud of you girls pursuing your dreams," Mommy said surprising both of us. We looked at each other and smiled. Our daddy stormed out the room in rage. "Give him some time to calm down."

"You're really okay with this?" Asia asked her.

"You two have always been rebellious. I'm not surprised you want to decide your own destiny."

"Thank you, Mommy," we said at the same time running over and giving her hugs and kisses.

We sat and talked with our mother about our plans to open a salon together. Asia will be doing hair; while I do makeup. It will be a full-service salon with manicures, pedicures and massages. Even though, our father was upset, I felt great leaving my parent's house. I was ready to start investing in my dream. I was so excited about opening our business. I went home and popped a bottle of wine. I grabbed my laptop and sat down on the sofa to start doing some research. I flipped on the television and started searching the web until television caught my attention. The news reporter mentioned Randall's name. I turned it up. It seemed a sex tape had surfaced of him on the internet. I hurriedly typed in his name. I burst into laughter. Randall was in leather bondage with a gag in his mouth. He was being spanked by a female with a leather mask on. That wasn't the funny part. The female put on a strap on and fucked him. I was in tears from laughing so hard. *Drea is a damn fool!*

Riley

"What's up fella?" Asia said walking up to our table in my bar. We were all out celebrating our new connect and avenging the Santiago family's murder. The only thing not going good in my life is Tawny and me. I've been back a week since our trip to Mexico, but still haven't reached out to her.

"What's up future wife?" Orpheus said licking his lips at her. She rolled her eyes and ignored him.

"So y'all damn near kill each other a few days ago. Now, y'all best friends," she said looking at Tone and me. We both shrugged our shoulders.

"Well, I just wanted to stop and speak." She looked at Max and turned her nose up. "Good to see the scratches healing well."

"Fuck you Asia, with them big ass feet," Max said looking down at her feet.

"Nigga, my feet ain't big. I wear a size nine," she said bobbing her head.

"Stop lying! Her lil ass flopping around here with a size eleven shoe like you got on scuba diving shoes," he said making us laughed. She stormed off.

"Do you annoy everybody?" Orpheus asked him.

"Not my fault, they overly sensitive," he said shrugging her shoulders.

"Well, lay off my future wife," Orpheus said standing up from the table.

"I'm bout to get up outta here," Tone said standing.

"Ok, best friend. Holla at me tomorrow," Max said smiling up at Tone. Tone shook his head and I chuckled at Max annoying ass.

I was surprised to see Tawny and Lexi walk into the bar. Max and I just looked at each other. She looked damn good. She was wearing a white, sleeveless dress that stopped midway her thick ass thighs. The dress was gripping every curve in her body. Her breast was pushed together sitting up like two melons. My dick jumped at the thought of what I wanted to do to her. She had her hair up in a high ponytail that hung down her back. Her and Lexi made their way to a table. I always have live musicians before ten on Friday nights. They took a table in front of the stage to enjoy the music.

"I'm out," Max said getting up from the table.

"You not gone holla at Lexi?" I asked.

"Nah, she said all we needed to say to each other," he said before walking away.

I sat back and watched them turn down man after man. I sat there and took it long as I could. I had to have her. I made my way over to their table. "Get up," I demanded staring down at her.

"Well damn, hello to you too," Lexi said sarcastically. I gave her a nod, never taking my eyes off Tawny.

"I'm not moving. Go find Sherry. I'm sure she wouldn't mind sucking your dick in the alley."

"You either get the fuck up or I'm dragging yo ass out of here."

"Riley, we have nothing to talk about. You said everything you wanted to say."

I leaned down and stared her in the eyes. "I'm going to say this one last time. Get the fuck up, Tawny." Her entire facial expression softened once she saw the seriousness in my face.

"I can't leave Lexi here by herself."

"Lexi need to get her ass up and go fix what's broken. Who drove?" I asked.

"I did," Tawny answered with an attitude.

"Give Lex your car keys and let's go," I said. She reluctantly gave Lexi the car keys and stomped out of the bar. "Lexi, go find my damn cousin."

She pouted the entire ride to my house. Once I was in my garage, I walked to her side of the car and opened the door. I wasn't arguing with her. I lifted her up throwing her across my shoulder. I carried her upstairs and threw her on the bed. I know there were a lot of things we needed to discuss, but I was thinking with my dick right now. I yanked her to the edge of the bed by his ankles. I spread her legs causing her dress to rise. I reached and snatched her panties off in one pull. I licked my lips as I stared at her fat, juicy, shaved pussy. I stared into her eyes. She was begging for me to taste her. Her chest heaved up and down. I kneeled resting her legs on my shoulders. The scent of her sweet aroma caused my dick to throb. I stroked my tongue over her juicy, wet pussy lips causing her body to tremble as she whimpered softly. Her thick sweet juices started to spill from between her lips. I used my fingers to part them leaving her wide open for me to enjoy. I covered her soaked pussy with my mouth, sucked and gulped her juices down my throat. She moaned out loud as her hips bucked from the sensations of feeling my wet, warm mouth on her sweetness. My tongue moved slow. I wanted to her to enjoy every stroke my tongue gave her. "Ooooohhh Ryyyy," she moaned as I licked, slurped, nibbled and sucked on her. I flicked my tongue across her clit. She gripped my head pressing my mouth deeper inside her, until she baptized me with her essence. I licked up, down, side to side while her body stiffened and quivered. She screamed out her love for me, only causing me to want more of her. I pushed her knees up to her chest and tongued her leaking tunnel while I massaged her clit. I slid my tongue down to her ass making wet circles around her ass. She was so damn sweet I buried my entire face between her ass cheeks determined not to let a spot go untouched my tongue. She was squirting, cussing and crying while I enjoyed what I've missed so much. I licked and slurped until she was clean as she whimpered and shook. I stood up and removed my clothes and hers. She looked so damn sexy laying there for my pleasure. I leaned over her, and she pressed my head forward devouring my mouth. Our tongues wrestled inside each other's mouth as my hands fondled her succulent breast. I licked and kissed my way down to them biting and sucking on her nipples with just enough pressure. She lifted and spread her legs grabbing them by the ankles. She wanted me inside her as bad as I wanted to be there. Her glossy, wet pussy was dripping her juices on the mattress. I placed the head my dick at her entrance. "Aaaaaahhhh," I groaned as I slid inside her. She pinned her legs on the side of her head giving me complete control. She didn't want it slow and easy. She wanted me to fuck her until I couldn't. I gripped her waist slamming my dick inside over. Gushing and slapping sounds echoed over the room as I hammered inside her. "Who pussy, Tawny?" I asked as I continued to ram my dick as deep as I could inside her. Her eyes were rolled back with her mouth open as she exploded soaking the bed. "Who got damn pussy this is?" I asked again breaking each word down with a pump inside her tight, wet tunnel.

"It's yours Ry! It's always been yours baby!" She screamed as she came again. "Oh God! I can't stop coming!"

"This pussy so damn good!" I roared as I felt my nuts swell and tingling sensations going through my body. "Hold it for me, baby. I want you to come with me." I started plummeting in and out faster and harder until my toes curled up. "Gggggggrrrrr!" I roared like a bear releasing inside her. She came with me unable to move as her sweet juices sprayed from my stomach running down my thighs. "Sssshhhit!" I barked as I kept coming unloading inside her.

Max

I don't know why she's still here. There's no forgiving her for what she did. I'm sure the only reason she's still here, because she is broke. I will make sure she doesn't get one brown penny from me or Granny. I'm sure she's planning to ask Granny for some more money, if she hasn't already. It'll be a cold day in hell before she gets another brown penny from me or Granny. She's lucky I'm allowing her to eat and sleep at my Granny's house. I wanted to send her ass back to California with her broke ass husband, but to make Granny happy I kept my mouth shut. She's been calling my phone since I got back from Mexico. I've ignored all her calls. After leaving the bar, I went home, took my pain pills and crashed on the sofa.

I felt touches on my back and immediately sat up ready to kill somebody. Lexi was kneeled in front of the sofa. "What you doing here, Lexi?" She stayed kneeled between my legs looking up at me.

"I'm sorry, Max. I didn't mean anything I said."

"We good," I said attempting to stand up. She placed her hands on my thighs to keep me seated.

"Ugh!" I groaned from the pain from the gunshot wound.

"What's wrong?" She asked. She lifts my basketball shorts to see the bandage around my thigh. "What happened?"

I chuckled. "King shot me."

"What?" She asked with wide eyes.

I smiled. "We were playing cops and robbers."

"Really Max? The bandages look like they need changing," she said getting up off the floor. She left the room and came back with the bandages to redress my wound. She fussed while she worked on my thigh. Accusing us of being over grown kids and playing dangerous games. I smiled to myself looking at her pretty face. She had her hair pulled up in a messy bun. She was wearing a pair of yoga pants and tee shirt, but she couldn't have looked more beautiful if she was wearing a thousand-dollar dress and her face was made up.

"Better?" She asked looking at me.

"Yea."

She sat next to me. "I didn't mean those things Maxwell. I just wanted you to feel how I was feeling. Drea told me what was going on. I was wrong and I'm sorry." They fired Randall and he dropped out the race. I heard he was beaten and had one of his hands cut off. I don't know how true it was.

I laughed. "Did you see the video?" I laughed shaking my head yes. I stared at her. "I wanna fuck the shit out of you right now." She giggled, but right now I wanted to kill King for handicapping me.

"I can take care of you," she said massaging my hard dick through my shorts.

I smiled at her ready to feel her lips around my dick. Just when she started pulling my dick out my phone started ringing. I would've answered the call if it wasn't my Granny's phone number. She would never call me after eleven o'clock at night. I answered the call.

"Baby, can you come to the ER?" She asked. I panicked and jumped up dropping the phone. I grabbed Lexi's hand and my keys on the way out the door.

I broke the speed limit and ran every light rushing to the hospital. I parked in front of the ER and rushed inside. I was surprised to see my Granny sitting in the waiting room. I walked over to her looking at her to see what was wrong with her. I didn't see any physical injuries. "It's your mother." Heat ran through my body. If I had none it was her, I would be getting my dick sucked right now.

"Granny, that's not my problem," I said looking at her.

"What's wrong with her, Ms. Violet?" Lexi asked standing beside me.

"She tried to kill herself. She took a lot of pills," Ms. Violet said as tears slid down her cheeks. Regardless, she was still her daughter and I know she loves her. I knew it was her way of getting attention. She used to do that shit with my old man. He'll feel sorry for her and act right for a few days. She knew the right amount to take.

"She just wants sympathy. She's not getting any from me," I said walking off.

"Maxwell," Lexi said calling my name.

I turned to face her. "Call and let me know if she dies." I left Lexi there with my Granny. Not only was she causing shit to resurface that I wanted to forget, she was bringing stress to my

Granny. I just wanted her to get out of our lives. My life was good before she decided to come back begging for money. It was a couple more hours before Lexi came back in the house. I was laying in the bed watching television. I didn't know if she would come back, but I was hoping she would. She removed all her clothes and slid into bed. She cuddled against me placing her head on my chest.

"You have to forgive her Maxwell. Not for her, but for you. I didn't realize how much hate you have for you until now. You don't care if she lives or dies," she said.

I sat up in the bed resting my back on the headboard. She sat up beside me. "He beat me until I was unconscious sometimes. My back is covered in scars from him tying me to the bed on my stomach and whipping me with a belt. I couldn't understand why he hated me so much. After he beat me, he would smoke a cigarette while I cried. Once he was done, he would put the cigarette out on my back or stomach. I begged him to kill me sometimes. She left me there knowing what would happen. I heard him on the phone with her one day. He told her he was going to beat the shit out of me until she comes back. I was scared, but happy. I knew since he told her that she was coming back. She never did. He came home sloppy drunk one night with some women. He tried to make me have sex with her. I'm not gone lie I was excited. I was twelve about to get my first piece of pussy until he sat in a chair and pulled out his dick. I took the lamp on the night stand and knocked him across the head. He was so drunk, he couldn't get up. I kicked and stomped him until I was tired. I ran out of the house never looking back."

I turned my head to look at Lexi's blood shot eyes and wet face. "How the fuck do I forgive that. I wanted to die. I felt like I wasn't worth the dirt I walked on."

"Maxwell, look at what you endured. They bruised and scarred you physically and emotionally, but they didn't break you. You didn't want to die, you wanted to escape. You fought back and won. You are a strong, successful man with a good heart. Yes, it's damaged but not broken. You don't feel like you can give love, because of them. You have to let the hate go. I'm not saying have her in your life, but forgive her."

He chuckled. "I guess it' s kinda like the quote. "Life becomes easier when you learn to accept the apology you never got."

"That's true," she said.

"I'm sorry Lexi. For all the fucked-up shit I've ever did to you. I love everything about you. You got my soul girl," he said.

She smiled. "I love you too Maxi Pooh."

"Now, if you ever tell anyone I was pouring my heart out to you like this I'm denying that shit and killing you." She burst into laughter as I wiped the tears from her face.

"I finally told my parents about my job and started my own business," she said with pride.

"How did they take it?" I asked. I was happy she finally decided to stand up to her father. She deserved the life she wanted to live, not the one he wanted for her.

"He's not talking to me right now. Our mother surprised me by being excited." She talked for hours about her and Asia opening a salon. I just sat and listened to all the ideas she had for their new business.

Tawny

"I see you happy again. Which one you choose the crack head or the drug dealer?" Ms. Daisy asked me as I drove her from grocery store.

"Max is not a drug dealer and Tone is no longer doing drugs. They both are successful business men," I told her pulling into her drive way.

She was starting to annoy me with her disrespect about Max and unwanted opinion about my life. I love her and everything that she has done for me, but I don't need her telling me how to live my life. I sped up to get her home quicker. Soon as I pulled into the drive way I jumped out the car to start unloading her grocery. Once I had them all in the house, I started putting everything away.

"Why don't you stay and eat dinner with me?" She asked as I hurriedly put the groceries away. "I can make your favorite, chicken and dumplings." As good as that sounded there was no way I was going to sit down with her and listen to her disrespect the man that I love."

"That's sounds delicious, but Riley and I have dinner reservations," I lied.

"Oh ok, I just get lonely in this big house. I hardly see you since you got a boyfriend." Now, I felt bad. I haven't been coming around much as I usually did. It's not that I didn't want to. I just get tired of her telling me about my poor choices in men. I took a deep breath.

She's been good to me over the years. I don't know where I would be without her.

"I can stay. I'll just take Riley a plate. I can stay here, and we can cook together," I said with a smile.

She rolled her eyes at me. "Tell him I season my food. I know white people like bland food. I don't play that in my kitchen." I had to giggle. You couldn't tell her Riley wasn't white. I called him to let him know I was going to help her cook dinner and will bring him a plate. I wanted to tell him about the baby last night after he sexed me to sleep, but something wouldn't let me. I don't know why I'm so scared of letting him in to help me with my success. I just don't see how I can run two studios, raise a baby and be a wife to him also. If my job required sitting behind a desk, I could do it. I'm a dancer that gives three to four classes a day. I would have to take time off during the pregnancy, after and not to mention getting my body back in shape.

I helped Ms. Daisy cook my favorite meal. She sang while she cooked. She has a beautiful voice. She started cleaning the chicken while I chopped vegetables. The smell of the raw meat made me nauseous. My stomach started to turn, and mouth watered. I felt the bile coming up through my throat and ran to the bathroom. I vomited until nothing, but water was coming up. I grabbed a toothbrush from one of the drawers and brushed my teeth. I walked back out to the smell of the chicken still making me sick.

"You okay?" She asked.

"Yes ma'am. Must be a virus or something," I lied. There was no way I was telling her I was pregnant.

She scoffed and shook her head. "Chile, I'm an old woman. I know a pregnant woman when I see one."

"What? I'm not pregnant."

"Don't lie to me Tawny Marie Andrews," she demanded. I knew when she said my full name she meant business. Even though I was a grown woman now, I still held the upmost respect for her. It was something about the tone of her voice that put you in your place. She didn't have to scream or cuss for you to know that she wasn't to be played with.

"Yes, I'm pregnant," I said shamefully.

"Stupid! Just plain ol' stupid!" She spat stomping her feet.

"I'm not stupid. I'm pregnant from a man that loves me and will do anything to make me happy." This is why I didn't want her to know. I knew she would make me feel horrible for being pregnant. I wasn't sure how I felt about having this baby yet, but she was going to make me feel like this was the worst thing I've ever done.

"You just like yo mama. Young and dumb. That boy is doing everything to hold you back and you falling for it," she said.

I was confused by her statement. She never knew my mother. My mother was from Reno. That was where I was born. "You didn't know her, to judge her. I'm the one that was left alone with no supervision, not you." I was started to get emotionally.

"Let me tell you something. I know everything about your family. You are following in your mother's footsteps and don't even know it. Your grandmother was my best friend. She raised your mother and she got a full scholarship because she was just that smart. She went off to college and got tied up with some drug dealer. Her grandmother went broke sending her to expensive rehabs only for her to go crawling back to that man. She ran your grandmother to an early grave with a stroke. She poured her heart out to me over the phone many of nights about Tracey's addiction. I promised her I would do all I could to look after you and I did, from a distance. When I found out she was leaving you unattended, I was the one who called social services," she ranted.

I was stuck. I couldn't believe she knew my mother and grandmother this entire time. I stood there with tears running down my face. "Why didn't you tell me?"

"For what? You didn't need to know how bad your mother was on that stuff. Yo daddy was killed for messing up somebody's drugs. She overdosed shortly after. I promised myself I would raise you to never fall for a man's bullshit. Everything I've ever taught you, all the hard work you did to get where you are; has been destroyed. Now you got to depend on a man to make sure you succeed," she said shaking her head. I couldn't stand to hear another word. I snatched my keys off the counter and ran out the house thinking I've made the worst mistake of my life getting pregnant.

Lexi

"King find you a spot yet?" Max asked as I lounged on couch watching him play video games. We hadn't been out the house in two days. Maxi was in her room playing. I loved being here when he has her over. I feel like we are a family.

"No, I'm getting aggravated," I answered.

"Don't rush it. I guess he's just looking for the perfect spot. You know it has to be in the right location," he said.

"I guess."

"I gotta take Maxi home. You riding with me?" He asked turning the game off.

"Yes, put some clothes on. I want to take you somewhere with me after we drop her off," I said throwing the cover back.

He looked at me curiously. "What kind of clothes?" I told him to dress casually. I wasn't telling him until I got him in the car, that we were going to my parent's house for dinner. I know if I tell him now, he won't go. I offered to drive, so he would have to go since we were in my car. I know he was going to be mad. I figured I'll make it up to him later today. After dropping Maxi off, we headed to my parent's house. My father was still mad at us, but our mother wanted us to come over for dinner. Our oldest sister and her family was in town. She wanted all of us to sit down and enjoy dinner together. I wasn't sure how this was going to go.

We pulled into the driveway of my parents' house. "Where we at?" He asked looking at the house.

I smiled at him. "My parents' house." I didn't wait for his reply. I hurried out of the car. He was calling my name as I continued to walk toward the house. Once I got on the porch, I turned to see him approaching me slowly with a frown on his face.

"I'm fucking yo lil ass into a coma when we get back to my place," he said walking up the steps. I giggled. When he approached me, I tiptoed to kiss his lips. He stared down at me. He leaned down to meet my lips. "You didn't have to do this." He said after breaking our kiss.

"I'm not doing it for you. I'm doing it for me," I said with a smile. I used my key to unlock the door. No one ever sits in my parents' living room, so we walked down the hall to the den. My parents, oldest sister, her husband and daughter were sitting and talking.

"Hey baby, I'm glad you made it," Mommy said getting up walking toward me. She gave me a tight hug as I hugged her back. "Oh my, I didn't know you were bringing a guest." I saw Daddy turn to look over his shoulder. He looked Max up and down.

"Mommy this is Maxwell, my boyfriend."

"Hi, young man. It's nice to meet you. I had no idea my baby had a boyfriend," Mommy said smiling and shaking Max's hand.

"It's a pleasure to meet you. Lexi surprised me by bringing me here. I hope I'm not intruding," Max said.

"Oh no, we are happy to have you. Any friend of Lexi's more than welcome," Mommy said. I introduced him to the rest of the family. My daddy didn't say anything to him. He barely spoke to me. I knew Max didn't take it personal, because he knew he was mad at me for not wanting the career he chose for me. Max was talking sports with Kendall, my sister's husband while I talked with Amarie about our new business venture and her job. Their four-year-old daughter was asleep in Daddy's lap. It was almost dinner time and I started to wonder where Asia was. She told me she was coming. A few minutes later, Mommy announced it was dinner time. Max followed me upstairs to my old room to wash our hands. Mommy cooked a pot rot with potatoes and carrots, rice, cabbage, mac and cheese and cornbread.

"I don't know where your sister is. She said she was coming," Mommy said referring to Asia. Asia was very carefree. She was far more rebellious than me. She would get me into a lot of trouble when we were younger, following her.

"I tried calling her again. She didn't answer," Amarie replied.

"She'll show up later looking for a doggy bag," Mommy said.

"So, what do you do Maxwell?" Daddy asked. *Here it goes.* I thought to myself.

"I own a few businesses," Max answered. "A club, restaurants, car washes, convenience stores."

"Oh wow, that's impressive," Mommy said smiling at Max. Daddy nodded his head. I don't think he was expecting that answer from Max. He started asking Max all kinds of questions about his background. Max remained calmed and answered all his questions. He was honest and straightforward about his past. I was surprised when he told me about his time in prison. My Daddy surprisingly never flinched a muscle. I just knew he was about to go ballistic.

"I'm impressed young man. A lot of young men would have used their prison time as an excuse for their failures. You used them as a motivation," Daddy said. Max nodded his head at him. I couldn't stop the big grin from spreading across my face as I look up at Max. He placed his hand between my thighs under the table. I know he could feel the heat coming from my moist mound. He looked at me and winked his eye.

"I couldn't give up. I knew there was something in the future waiting for me," he said staring at me and gently squeezing my thigh. Daddy smiled and nodded his head.

I leaned over and whispered in his ear. "That was corny as fuck." He laughed.

"I'm sorry I'm late," Asia walked into the kitchen. I was shocked to see Orpheus standing behind her.

"At least you made it," Mommy said standing up. "Well, I guess you have a boyfriend too?"

Asia giggled. "Not exactly, he's my husband." She stood there with a big smile on her face while all our mouths dropped open. Max burst out laughing. Mom flopped back down in her chair. My dad stood up in a fit of rage.

Max

"Man, thank you for taking the heat off me," I said laughing at Orpheus as we stood in the living room. We could hear yelling coming from the kitchen. Asia's father was giving her hell.

"What kind of stupidity have you two done?" Lexi's older sister asked staring at Orpheus. He just stared straight through her with no reply.

"Orpheus is she serious. You two really go married?" Lexi asked him. He smiled and nodded his head.

"Man, how you gone go marry her. Her feet are like fins," I laughed. "You married Ariel, the mermaid."

"I know, her shit is magical," he said with a smile. I laughed harder.

"Shut up Maxwell, this is not a laughing matter. My father is going ham in there," Lexi said in frustration. I tried to stop laughing.

"Yo, this their problem. We got business to handle at my place. Let's roll," I said staring at Lexi.

"I can't leave my sister here alone."

"Shit, he ain't gone kill her. Besides she's got a husband to defend her now," I said with a smile.

"Amarie, tell Asia to please call me when everything calms down." Her sister nodded her head in agreement.

She looked at Orpheus. "You are unbelievable."

"Goodnight sis," Orpheus yelled as Lexi stormed out the house. I followed behind her. She ranted all the way to the house. I sat quietly and listened until we pulled into my driveway.

"Aren't you upset about this?" She asked as we sat in the car.

"Nah Lexie, that's their business. They're both grown. Some people don't need years to decide to build a life together. If it doesn't work, so what? Now, what we're not going to do, is take this shit in the house with us. Leave that shit out here. I'm taking you in this house, eating the fuck out my pussy and then fucking you to sleep." All she did was look at me and smile.

We started tearing each other's clothes off the moment we stepped into the house. "The entire time we were eating dinner, I was picturing her naked on the dining room table." I took her by the hand taking her to my dining room. I sat her up on the tall table spreading her legs wide. This wasn't going to be slow, sweet love making. I wanted hot, passionate fucking. I dove inside her sweet dripping pussy twirling my tongue round and round, up and down, licking, slurping and sucking. She was moaning and whimpering as I grunted and groaned, as I devoured her sweetness. "Maaaxxxx!" She screamed out as I used my tongue on her swollen, pulsating clit. She gripped the back of my head as she came. Her cream covered my mouth dripping down my chin. She collapsed on the table. I licked and slurped while her body quivered. I pinned her knees against her chest lapping my tongue from the pussy to her ass. "Oooohhhh sssshhhit!" she moaned as I stuck my tongue in her ass while sticking two fingers in her creamy tunnel. "Oooohhh I'm bout to come!"

"Mmmmmm," I groaned as I continued to satisfy her ass and pussy. Her juices were seeping from her pussy down to her ass, and I wasn't missing a drop. I pressed my fingers against her g-spot sending her over the edge again. She released so hard her cream splattered on the table. Her sweet skin was covered in sweat. I stood up stroking my throbbing dick. In one stroke I was deep inside her pressing against her spot. She moaned out her ecstasy as she lifted her upper body off the table. She wrapped her arms around me tightly. She was coming on my dick as it pumped inside her. "You love me Lexi?" I asked as I nibbled on her earlobe.

"Yes Max, I love you so much." I lifted her from the table still deep inside her. I walked over and pinned her against the wall. I started drilling like I was trying to find the richest oil. I licked and sucked her sweet, sweaty skin while massaging her perfect breast. She was coming over and over. My thigh was in a lot of pain, but I didn't give a fuck. Being inside her was worth all the pain I was feeling. Our bodies were dripping in sweat as I continued to give her what we both craved. I brushed her hair out her face with my hand. Her eyelids were low as she stared at me.

"I swear I love you," I said staring back at her. She was my everything. She clinched her muscles around my dick and started twirling her hips. "Ffffuuuck! Aaarrrggghhh!" I howled as we both came together. I kept her pinned against the wall until I gained full mobility in my legs. I pecked her on the lips. "That's that "act right."

She laughed as she rested her head on my shoulder. The rest of the night was no different. I know my thigh was going to be sure as hell tomorrow, but I didn't care. She was worth it.

Natavia Presents

Riley

"Stop it! You're going to make me pee on myself," Tawny laughed as we played in her bed. She had called me to come over, because she was upset about an argument with her Godmother. That was one mean, grouchy old lady. After taking her out to eat, we fucked each other to sleep. Now, I was trying to make her get up and get ready to go to her studio. She was being lazy.

She sat up in the bed and looked at me. "Lexi and Tamara are handling classes today. I have a doctor's appointment."

"You okay?" I asked worriedly.

"Yea, I'm just pregnant," she said not seeming to be happy about it.

"What?" I asked to make sure. My heart felt like it was going to explode with joy.

"I'm pregnant Ry," she said getting out the bed. I couldn't stop the grin on my face. It disappeared when I looked at her. "This a problem for you?"

"Yes, it's a problem. I can't teach classes pregnant. I wanted to open a new studio. How can I do all that and pregnant?" She asked with an attitude.

It felt like fire ran through my body. I got out the bed, walked to her side of the bed and stared down at her. "You don't want our child?"

Natavia Presents

She became nervous. "It's just bad timing. I want a family with you. I just wanted to do other things first."

It takes a lot for me to lose my temper. Right now, it was out the damn window. "Kill my child and I will fucking kill you." I know it's a woman's right to choose and I respect that. I just don't understand how a woman wouldn't want to have a baby with a man that would do anything to see she is happy.

"I want to have this baby, Riley. I promise I do, but I'm scared," she said as water filled her eyes.

"Scared of what?" I asked angrily.

"I'm scared of losing myself. I don't want to wake up one day and realize, I didn't do what I wanted with my life," she said.

I took a deep breath to calm down. "Do whatever you need to do, Tawny. If you can't trust me to lead you forward, I ain't the nigga for you. I'm not an insecure nigga. I'm not the type of man to hold a woman back to make myself feel like a man. I'm the type to lead her to her goals. If you don't know that shit by now, you'll never know it."

"I do trust you."

"Nah baby girl, you don't. If you did, you wouldn't be scared to have our child. You wouldn't think twice about being my wife," I told her.

"What's wrong with wanting to accomplish my goals first?"

"Why do you need to do it alone?"

"So, I'll know it's mine. I want to have something I know I'll never lose," she said in tears.

I scoffed. "Like I said, you don't trust me."

"Ry, where are you going?" She asked as I walked to her door.

I turned to face her. "Let me know what you decide to do about the baby. It's your body, your choice."

I left to check on the streets and businesses. I've done all I could to convince her I would be there for her. I don't doubt her love for me. The problem with her is; she doesn't know how to let a man be a man for her. I would never hold her back. Shit, if she wanted to run for president I'll be right there by her side. I can't convince her of that. She must trust and believe I would be there for her.

"You got a nerve showing up here. I haven't seen or heard from you since you been fucking Tawny," Anita said opening her door. She was right. I haven't fucked with anyone since Tawny. I don't even know what I was doing at her door, now. After the blow up with Tawny, I drove until I ended up knocking on her door.

"You gone let me in or not?" I asked. I really didn't give a damn if she did or didn't. She swung the door open and let me in. She stood there with her arms crossed over her chest with an attitude as I walked in. She was thick in all the right places standing there in a pair of Pink boy shorts and tank top. I walked in and sat down on the sofa.

"What do you want, Riley?" She asked walking toward me.

"What have I always come here for?" I asked staring at her thick thighs and fat pussy that was trying to rip through the shorts.

"What's in it for me?" She asked with a sexy grin.

"Some good dick." She giggled and straddled my lap. She started gyrating her hips and kissing on my neck. I couldn't even bring myself to touch her. My dick was thinking for my heart, but my mind was thinking about Tawny. She tried to kiss me, but I turned my head. She reached down and pulled out my dick.

"Damn, I miss this big mothafucka," she said as she stroked me with her hand. "I knew she didn't know what to do with all this. It takes more than one woman to satisfy all this."

I gripped her wrist and my dick softened in her hand. "Nah, this ain't happening. My bad," I said pushing her off my lap.

"Are you fucking serious, nigga?" She asked with an attitude.

I chuckled. "Yea, you fucked the mood up mentioning her with my dick in your hand."

"So, what? If the bitch was doing her job, you wouldn't be here."

"Nah if she wasn't doing her job, my dick would be down your throat right now." I stood up stuffing my dick back in my boxers. "You be good." I walked out relieved I didn't make shit worse than it already is.

Tawny

It's been almost two weeks since Riley walked out my house. He hasn't called or answered any of my calls or texts. I thought the least he would do was check on our baby. I was only a few weeks pregnant and morning sickness was whooping my ass. I couldn't stand the smell of raw meat. I hadn't been to Ms. Daisy's house since she told me who she was. I wasn't angry with her for keeping the secret. I just didn't want to hear her go on about my pregnancy.

"What's wrong?" Jiera asked as I stood to her door in tears. She pulled me in the house and hugged me as I sobbed like a baby.

"I lost him, Jay," I said as I cried.

"What happened?" She asked breaking our embrace. I stood there in tears telling her everything that happened. "You know I love you like a sis, Tawny but he's right. If you want to do it all on your own, what are you with him for?"

"Because I love him."

"You love him because you know he's a good man that provides, protects and loves you too. So, what's so hard about sharing your growth with him?"

"I don't know. I guess listening to all the shit Ms. Daisy said scares me."

"And look at her, miserable, grouchy and mean as hell," she said laughing. I laughed with her. "Come on, I'm in the kitchen cooking."

"Oh God no, this baby doesn't do raw meat," I said turning my nose up.

"Well, go in the den. Let me put it in the oven and I'll be in there in a minute." I did as she said and sat in the den. I was craving a glass of wine. The way I was feeling I could drink an entire bottle. I sat scrolling through my phone when Tone came walking into the den. I hadn't spoken with him since that day we met for drinks. That was our goodbye.

"What's up Tawny?" He asked flopping down on the sofa.

"Hi."

"What you crying about? I need to kill that nigga for you?" He asked smiling.

"No, I need for you two to keep doing what you are doing…acting like grown ass men," I said rolling my eyes. He laughed.

"Seriously, what's going on?" He asked staring at me.

I shook my head. "Nothing, just overwhelmed."

"Listen Tawny, I heard the things he said to you that night, about your independence. He's right. I remember you being too strong when we were together. You were always trying to lead. I'm not blaming that on my fuckups. I did those on my own. At the time, I didn't mind you leading, because I would've led you down a dead end. If I was the man I am now, the way you felt the need to do it all on your own wouldn't fly."

"Am I that bad?" I asked in disbelief.

He nodded his head. "Yea, you made every decision without consulting me. I remember wanting to keep your car detailed and tuned up, you choose to take it yourself. You remember that morning your tire was flat? Instead of coming back in the apartment and telling me to come change it, you tried doing the shit yourself."

"Because we had just gotten into a fight," I reminded him.

"Regardless, as your man I would never have you out there changing a damn tire. You didn't even know what the fuck you were doing," he said.

I sat there in deep thought. Neither one of us spoke until I looked at him. "I'm pregnant." A big smile appeared on his face.

He smiled. "Congratulations. You'll be a great mom."

I smiled. "I would, wouldn't I?" I said nodding my head. He laughed. "Yea, I like this new you."

He laughed. "Thanks, I do too."

"I gotta get out of here. Let me go tell Jay bye," I said getting up of the sofa. I went and told Jay I was leaving and headed to Riley's house.

I used my key to let myself in. It was made way to through the house bout I couldn't find him. I walked to the back of the house to see him relaxed in the hot tub. I stood there removing all my clothes as I admired his muscular chest and arms. I slid the door back and our eyes met. He just stared at me as I walked toward him praying I wasn't too late to correct my wrongs. He kept his eyes on me as I stepped down and straddled his lap. "I'm sorry. I want this baby and us. I want you to be the one that leads me. I don't want to do it alone or with anyone else. Can I be your wife?"

"Are you going to honor and obey?" I nodded my head yes. "Well, slide that good pussy down on my dick." I giggled and did what he asked. He slid his tongue in my mouth. I could taste the Cognac and cigar he was smoking on his sweet breath.

We made love in the hot tub and ended up in the bedroom. "How's my lil man doing in there?" He asked as we lay in his bed.

"He's annoying. I hope he doesn't act like Max," I said. He laughed. "It might be a girl."

"Nah, that's my lil man, but I'd be happy to have a little you running around," he said tapping me on my ass.

"I guess postponing my studio for a year isn't bad," I said.

"You don't have to do that. You are the damn boss. Hit up these strip clubs. Find some dancers that are willing to make some extra cash for a couple of hours a day. You can manage both studios yourself with an assistant manager. When the baby comes, Mama will be happy to babysit. I'll even let the ol' grouch keep my baby sometimes. Maybe that'll help soften her," he said smiling.

The way he was telling me, this could possibly work. I don't know why I made something so simple so complicated. I told him everything that happened between me and Ms. Daisy. I trusted Riley not to do the things that men did to my mother and her. I knew he loved me enough to always be there for me. I kissed my way down his chest until I was licking the crown of his meaty dick. The veins of his dick were etched in his shaft like bolts of lightning. My wet, warm tongue licked up and down his shaft. I slid my lips over his dick slurping it in and out of my mouth. "Mmmmmm," I moaned as saliva ran from my mouth, down his dick to his balls. I dipped down gently sucking them into my mouth.

"Ssssssss," he groaned gripping a handful of my hair. I massaged his balls inside my mouth with my tongue as I stroked his dick with my hand. I went back to his dick to see the pre-cum oozing out. My tongue made circular motions around the head savoring the taste of him. I slid him all the way in my mouth. I could feel the head of his dick hitting my throat. I sucked him in and out as he groaned from the pleasure my mouth was giving him. "Got damn! Shit I'm bout to come!" He roared giving me motivation to go faster. "Gggggrrrrrrr Sssshhhhhit!" He growled unloading in my mouth. I sucked him down my throat as his legs trembled and body jerked. The next morning there was a huge diamond sitting on my finger. All I could do was look at it and smile. Riley was still sleep. I snuggled against him relieved knowing, I have a man that loved me beyond measure.

<u>Lexi</u>

"Why haven't you called me? Where have you been?" I asked Asia as we sat in her living room.

"I've been on my honeymoon," she answered with a big grin on her face.

"You don't even know that man, Asia," I told her. She was acting so nonchalant about agreeing to spend her life with a man she just met a few days ago.

"It just felt so right at the time. We were thinking about getting it annulled, but decided to give it a try. Lex, that man's dick is a true beast. Girl, I was climbing the damn walls."

"That is just too much damn information," I said turning my nose up.

"After everyone let, he sat down with Daddy and charmed the hell out of him," she said laughing. Things are getting better with Daddy and me. Asia and I had a heart to heart talk with him. He promised he would work on trying let us follow our own dreams and give us the love and attention he has for us. I knew he loved us. He just didn't think we had the ambition like our two older sisters. He realized we did have it, but it wasn' t what he wanted. He sat down and talked with me and Max about the plans me and Asia have. He still wasn't completely happy with my decision, but he was going to try to be understanding. I didn't even know if she was still going to stay here since her husband lives in California.

Natavia Presents

"What about our salon?" I asked.

"We' re still doing it. I told you we decided to take it slow. I know it's backwards as hell," she said laughing. "I'll go there sometimes, and he'll come here." She was grown, and it was her life. She seems to be happy and that is all that matters to me.

"Well, I got to get out of here. I have dinner reservations with Maxwell," I said standing up.

"Tell Radio, I said hi," she said walking me to the door.

"Oh, that's low!" I said laughing. They were forever cracking jokes on each other.

I hurried home to get dressed. I decided to wear a black spaghetti strap, knee length, bodycon Versace dress Maxwell had purchased for me a few months ago. I applied my makeup. I was pinning my hair up when Maxwell came into the bathroom. "Nah, I like it down." I smiled at him and started removing the pins. After I was done, I turned to face him.

"I was thinking about cutting it all off. I want a boy cut," I told him. He tilted his head, looking at me as if he was trying to picture me with a low cut.

"What the fuck I'm going to grip when I'm giving you the "act right" from the back?" I laughed and pushed him out the way. "For real though, I think that shit would be sexy as hell on you. You'll look like Stoney at the end of Set It Off. I giggled and blushed.

I didn't notice until I got in the car how nice he was dressed. Maxwell didn't dress up often. Tonight, he was rocking a nice a black Versace blazer with a colorful lining, a button down black shirt and slacks. He had on a pair of Ferragamo loafers, I purchased for his birthday. I had to smile to myself when I thought about the day I gave him his gift. He was mad, because he never dresses up. He normally wears jeans, fitted tees and sneakers. We argued for hours. I noticed lately he's been dressing up more. I guess he liked the new look. We pulled up to valet and exited the car. When we entered the restaurant, Max told the host that someone was waiting for us. I was shocked when he gave his mother's name. We followed the host to the table. He's mother was sitting there looking beautiful. She reminded me of Kimora Lee Simmons, just not as tall.

"I'm so happy you came," she said gleaming with joy. Max surprisingly pulled my chair out for me to sit down. Max was a lot of things, but never the type to pull out chairs. "Hi Lexi, you look beautiful. I think that wearing your hair pinned up would complete the dress more."

"Maxwell loves my hair down," I said smiling at her. "You are stunning yourself."

"Oh, thank you. You definitely want to keep your man happy," she said with a smile. "Maxwell, you are so handsome. I've never seen you dressed up."

"It's not something I do often," he said. The waiter came and took our drink orders. Maxwell ordered a bottle of wine for me and his mother.

We made small talk while eating dinner. She would ask him about his businesses. I could tell she was happy to be able to sit and have a conversation with him. I was proud of Max for trying to move past this. I could tell how uncomfortable he was. I couldn't believe it when she said how happy he was to get the invitation to dinner. I automatically thought she invited him. After the waiter cleared our dishes, Maxwell spoke.

"I invited you here to say what I've always wanted to say to your face. I survived what would normally kill someone. I got the love from Granny, that I should've gotten from you and him. I gave her every reason in the world to turn her back on me. I was so messed up when I came to live with her. I didn't give a damn about myself or no one else. She loved me through it all. I still didn't know how to love anyone besides her until my daughter came along. I would sit and hold her in my arms wondering how can any parent neglect, abuse or abandoned their child. I remember begging you to take us away from there, but you wouldn't. You said we couldn't afford to leave. Soon as you saw an escape, you left me behind like I was garbage. You can spend the rest of your life trying to justify your actions and I still wouldn't understand. For so many years, I wanted to know. It doesn't matter anymore. I'm releasing all that anger and hurt. I'm doing that for myself, Granny, Maxi and Lexi. I gave this girl every excuse in the world to walk out of my life, but she didn't. She saw something in me that I didn't see in myself. I'm not angry anymore. You can go in peace knowing I've forgiven you."

A tear slid from her cheek. "Is there any chance we can try to have a relationship?"

"I don't know. Right now, you aren't my concern."

She burst into tears. "Maxwell, I need your help. I have no money." *And there it is.* "I have nowhere to go."

"I'm sorry, but you have to find your way like I did. You ready Lexi?" He asked standing up. I stood up from my chair.

"Can I at least stay with my mother until I get on my feet?" She asked looking up at him.

"You are her child. I would never tell her you're not allowed there, but don't take her kindness for weakness. She's the only mother I know," he said. "If you need a job, I might can help in that area."

"Thank you," she said giving him a forced smile. He took me by my hand and lead me out the restaurant. The rest of the evening was us cuddled up on the sofa watching movies.

<u>Jiera</u>

"**I** hate to see you leave," I told Tone standing in our kitchen. We invited everyone over for Thanksgiving dinner. He would be returning to Minnesota in a couple of days.

"I promise, I'll be coming back more," he said. I couldn't fault him for staying in Minnesota now. He won a bid on a multi-million-dollar contract. I thought King had something to do with it, but he said he didn't. Regardless, my brother was now the man that raised me.

"You better. You guys are taking my niece away," I reminded him. "Plus, I gotta find someone to replace her at the store. I'm happy for you guys though."

"There goes my best friend," Max said walking into the kitchen. I laughed. He annoyed the hell out of Tone, but they have become good friends.

We never expected any of our lives to turn out this way. I couldn't be happier with the outcome. Max and Lexi are doing great. He's treating her like a queen. They've found a building to open their salon. Max surprised her by purchasing the building and hiring someone to decorate and furnish the entire salon. He gave his mother a job to help her get on her feet. He's working on developing a relationship with her. Tawny is finally letting Riley be the man in her life that he wants to be. She's moved in with Riley and their planning to marry in February. She's even convinced Ms. Daisy to give him a chance. Ms. Daisy came over for Thanksgiving too. She brought the best dressing I've ever tasted in my life. Angela teased her about finding her a boyfriend. That was the first time I've ever seen her laugh. As far as King and I, things have never been better. After saying good night to everyone, I started cleaning the kitchen.

"Nah, leave that shit. I'll call a cleaning service in the morning," King said walking up behind me.

"You sure?" I asked.

"Yea, Ma took lil man home with her. Come on, they finished with the room," he said smiling. I smiled at him. I took off running upstairs. He burst into laughter. I was disappointed to find the door locked. "King, come on. Hurry up! I wanna see!" I yelled jumping up and down. King was so mad the night Lexi and Max decided to make up in a private room one night after one of their numerous fights he refused to use it again. He hired someone to redo the entire room. He was taking his time walking up the stairs and I was getting very impatient.

"Cover your eyes," he ordered before unlocking the door. I covered them until I heard the door open. My mouth nearly hit the floor. The room was completely different. The only thing he kept was the stripper pole, the black walls and the stage name sign. The black walls were decorated with glowing stars to make it look as if it was night time. He installed a hanging bed with a skyline above it. The floors were black marble. There was a basin tub sitting on one side of the room. He had filled it with water and rose petals.

Flickering candles surrounded the room. He had a black sex bench at the foot of the huge bed. The comforter set was black and white.

"I love it," I said turning to face him. He picked up a remote control and Luke James' *Drip* played over the surround sound.

"Then why you still got on clothes?" He asked with a smile. He didn't have to tell me twice. I started tearing off clothes as I made my way to the tub. Once I was in, King came and sat behind me. My mouth watered at the sight of his chocolate, thick dick. I could feel it poking in my back as we lay in the tub.

"Why did you remove the bar?" I asked as we lay relaxed in the tub.

"Only thing I'm drinking from in this room is you," he said as he nibbled on my neck and my massaged my breast. He moved his hand down to my belly, to between my thighs. He stroked his fingers between my lower lips. Soft bites on my neck mixed with the massage he was giving my clit was driving me crazy. Suddenly, he stopped. "I want it in my mouth," he whispered in my ear.

I lifted my body out the tub. My legs were weak from the pleasure he was giving me before he stopped. He got out the tub with his dick pointing right at me. I couldn't resist him. Without saying a word, I dropped to my knees taking his brick hard dick in my mouth. "Damn Jiera!" He barked as I sucked him into my mouth. I used both my hands to massage his shaft while sucking on the head. I could feel his dick jumping in my hands. I slid down gently caressing his balls with my tongue. Pre-cum oozed from his dick and I couldn't let it go to waste. I sucked the head enjoying the taste of him. I wanted more, so I started sucking him faster and deeper. I gripped the back of his thighs as I bobbed up and down his shaft. Saliva poured from my mouth, only for me to slurp it back in on every stroke. I reached down and started massaging his balls. They were full of his sweetness, and I was ready for him to give it all to me. Faster, deeper and harder I sucked on his thick, long dick until he couldn't hold it any longer. His body stiffened and convulsed as he roared with ecstasy, unloading in my mouth. I sucked down every drop never removing him from my mouth. "Fuck!" He barked nearly losing his balance. He stumbled over to the bed and fell on his back. "Come sit that sweet pussy on my face." I did as I was told. I rotated my hips as I rode his face, while Alicia Keys and Maxwell serenaded us with *Fire We Make*. He ate me until I begged for mercy. My cream was sliding down the sides of his face before he was done. I lay on my back dizzy from the earth-shattering orgasms he had given me. He wasn't done. "Tasting you always makes my dick hard." He slid his massive dick inside me in one thrust. He stared down at me. "Damn, I fall in love with you more every day."

"I'll love you forever," I said as he slid in and out of me. The hanging bed rocked back and forth on his every stroke. He massaged, licked, sucked and nibbled on my breast while driving deep inside me over and over, until he hit my spot sending me into a galactic atmosphere. With the bed swaying, and mind-blowing orgasms, I felt like I was floating in a galaxy.

"Damn, this pussy gets better every time!" He groaned as he swelled inside me. He lifted my legs on his shoulder and started pounding inside me with no mercy. I loved the feeling of pain and pleasure he gives me. I could feel myself getting ready to come again.

"Ooooohhh King! I'm cooommming!" I screamed pouring my essence on us.

He thrust deep inside me. "Aaaarrrggghhhh!" He bellowed as he convulsed and trembled. He stayed there until his body relaxed. He collapsed on his back beside me.

"That's my little girl right there," he said smiling.

I laughed. "King, Mufasa isn't a year old yet. We'll work on one when he turns one."

"I'm unloading triplets in yo ass next time," he said pulling me in his arms. I burst into laughter. This was the life we all rebelled for.

THE END

Come find the author on Facebook @: Nona Day

Natavia Presents